JUST THEIR LUCK

A NOVEL BY

L.A. DONAHOE

www.firstchoicebooks.ca
Victoria, BC

Cover image by Debra Hughes, www.shutterstock.com (Image ID: 120742222)
Cover and layout design by Jenny Engwer, First Choice Books

Library and Archives Canada Cataloguing in Publication

Donahoe, L. A., 1959-, author
Just their luck : a novel / by L.A. Donahoe.

Issued in print and electronic formats.
ISBN 978-1-77084-585-5 (paperback).--ISBN 978-1-77084-636-4 (html)

I. Title.

PS8607.O624J88 2015 C813'.6 C2015-905466-4
C2015-905467-2

Printed in Canada ♻ on recycled paper

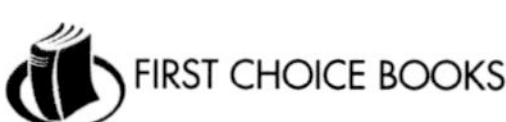

firstchoicebooks.ca
Victoria, BC

10 9 8 7 6 5 4 3 2 1

WITH LOVE

I would like to thank my amazing son P.J. Donahoe for faithfully encouraging me and supporting my efforts throughout the writing of my first novel.

Thank you to all my family and friends for your support and encouragement and a special thank you to the following for your valuable input and insight provided:

A. Bonner
G. "Bean" Warford
L.M. Watson
L. Whelan

ONE

The day had come for Sarah to leave. It was an unusually hot, sunny September morning and it was expected to get even warmer as the day went along. Walking down the front walkway towards her car, she sighed forlornly. Before leaving she had one last thing to do for Travis who was still asleep in the guest room upstairs. Quietly going into the garage, Sarah stood staring at Travis' pride and joy, his white BMW Z4 convertible with black leather interior. Travis had just washed and waxed the car by hand the day before and it sparkled.

She was sad thinking back to how they arrived at this day. Sarah and Travis had dated throughout University and moved to Watertown after graduation. Travis was drafted onto the Broncos Football team just before graduation and would be their star quarterback and Watertown was their home base. Travis begged Sarah to come with him. She agreed and that was a day she now regretted.

It hadn't been easy living in the same house with Travis recently. A couple of weeks ago Sarah decided to go visit her friend Chloe and thought she heard Travis' laughter while taking a shortcut through Morgan Park. At first she disregarded it because she knew that Travis was at practice that night and wasn't expected home until after eleven o'clock. His coach was pushing the team pretty hard leading up to the divisional championships and Travis was off to practice a lot. She knew how important winning the divisionals was to his career and never complained that he was gone more nights than he was home these last few months. What she didn't expect was to find Travis and Gretchen, a Broncos cheerleader, out together and it all went downhill from there. Travis swore he would stop seeing Gretchen, that he would do anything to get Sarah back, but Sarah's heart was broken. It was over and nothing could change that.

Now the day had finally arrived for her to leave and she felt that with all they had been through, the least she could do was write Travis a goodbye note and leave it on his car. So in black permanent marker and in large capital letters, Sarah wrote 'YOU'RE A CHEATING BASTARD TRAVIS!' on all four sides of his car. Admiring her work, Sarah smiled for the first time in days and as she left she tossed the marker on the floor of the garage.

"Go to hell you bastard!" With tears rolling down her cheeks, she hopped into her four-door Mustang convertible and headed out of town on the two-hour drive to her new life.

Sarah's sister Terri, a successful real estate agent in Forestville, had found a three-bedroom cottage on South Bay near Forestville that she felt was perfect for her younger sister. Sarah hadn't seen it yet but trusted that it was everything Terri had described to her. At this point in time, she really didn't care how the place looked, nor was she interested in any of the details. Terri had, however, told her that the house came partially furnished and so the fact that she had very little furniture to speak of and that the moving company wouldn't be delivering what belongings she did have to her new home for a couple of days, really wasn't going to be an issue. Sarah also knew she would need to get a job but felt comfortable that the little nest egg of cash she had saved would keep her cupboards full until she found work.

TWO

ARRIVING IN FORESTVILLE, SARAH KNEW to turn right at the gas station, head to Lakeshore Drive and then left to number 13692 and her new home. From what she could see as she drove through town there was a coffee shop/diner; a pharmacy; a mechanics shop/gas station; a fire hall and a pub on the left hand side of Main Street. On the right side was the medical centre consisting of a doctor and a dentist; a police station; a small movie theatre called "The Roxy"; (*weren't they all called that*, she thought); a grocery store and some other place with the windows all covered in paper. *Wow, I forgot how small Forestville was.*

Tired and distracted, Sarah missed her turn and decided to make a U-turn and double back. Not seeing a pick-up truck coming from the opposite direction, she crashed into the driver's side.

"Oh my God!" she shouted. Sarah couldn't believe what had happened. Getting out of her car, she quickly assessed that there was minimal damage, but enough that the driver of the other vehicle had to shove the door hard to get out of his truck. The driver was male, approximately six feet tall, with tussled dark, wavy hair that hung just below his ears and a well-built physique that Sarah found quite eye-catching. He was wearing slightly worn blue jeans, a gray t-shirt, sneakers, was carrying a well-worn cowboy hat and he had that unshaven look that was ever so sexy. Judging by the Forestville Fire Department sticker in his front windshield, she guessed that he was a firefighter. *Who doesn't like a firefighter? He really is good looking,* she thought with a smile. Self-consciously pushing her hair behind her ears, she watched him put his hat on and walk towards her. *As far as the male species goes, he is definitely an eight out of ten!*

"Lady, what in hell were you thinking when you made that U-turn? You must be the worst god-damned driver in the world!" he declared. "This is a brand new truck and you've managed to smash the door in with one idiotic move!"

Sarah was jerked from her pleasant thoughts, shocked by what she was hearing. Caught off guard she didn't quite know what to say. The eight out of ten quickly dwindled down to a three. *Who does he think he is calling me idiotic?* Sarah was enraged.

"Well, you don't have to be rude about it! It could've happened to anyone! It was an accident!" she yelled back.

"There was a driveway yards away from you, lady! You could have turned around there, but no, you had to make a bloody U-turn in the middle of the street, without looking I might add, and hit my brand new truck! This is all your fault, and you're paying for this!"

Sarah was not impressed with Mr. Gorgeous and his attitude, and proceeded to turn around and walk back to her car. Mr. Gorgeous followed after her, yelling, "Hey, where do you think you're going? I'm not finished with you yet!"

"Oh, but I'm finished with you!" Sarah replied with disdain. "I don't know who you think you are yelling at me this way, but I can assure you that I am done with this conversation. If you want to discuss this like a civilized human being, then you can come see me at 13692 Lakeshore Road!" The address just came out of her without thinking. With that, Sarah got into her car, leaving Mr. Gorgeous standing in the middle of the road with his mouth gaping, watching her drive away.

CHAPTER TWO

When she looked in her rear-view mirror, she could see him take his hat off and throw it on the ground in anger. *Wow! That guy was such a jerk! A good-looking jerk, mind you…but a jerk just the same. Welcome to Forestville, Sarah,* she thought with dismay as she drove away.

Just then, her cell phone rang. Seeing that it was Travis, she ignored it. She was in no mood to speak to him right now. After his third attempt at calling her, Sarah finally answered.

"Travis, I have no interest in speaking with you, so stop calling me!"

"You bitch, Sarah! What's the big idea of writing all over my car? You'll pay for this! You can count on that!" Travis was screaming from the other end of the phone.

Sarah was livid. "Go to hell, Travis! Let's not forget who cheated on whom! You got what you deserved!"

"People make mistakes, Sarah!" Travis yelled. It sounded so pathetic that this was all he could say about what he had done. In another time and place, he could have been talking about forgetting to take out the trash.

"Yeah, and I made the mistake of thinking I could trust you! You had your chance and you blew it! Don't ever call me again!" As she hung up the phone, tears started welling up in her eyes. She was shaken from the accident, and this conversation with Travis amplified her emotions. All Sarah wanted to do was get home. It had been a very long week and she was completely worn out.

THREE

WHAT THE HELL! LEFT STANDING in the middle of the road, Sam was in disbelief as he watched Sarah drive away.

Sam had heard that the Cudmores sold their place on Lakeshore Road and had moved to a condo in Lansdowne. His friend Terri was a real estate agent and mentioned that she had sold it, but she never elaborated as to who had bought it. Now he knew.

His week was getting worse as it went along. After having had a huge fight with his girlfriend and telling her she had to move out of his place and now this, Sam was getting real tired of all the drama.

He noted that the driver of the Mustang seemed to be about average height with shoulder-length dark brown hair that was wavy, yet slightly frizzy from the humidity of the day. She had dark brown eyes, tanned complexion and, in his opinion, could stand to lose a few extra pounds, but it certainly didn't take away from her attraction. She had a sex appeal that he hadn't seen around Forestville in a very long time. Although he felt his reaction was warranted, he was angry at the thought of losing his temper with the most beautiful brunette he had seen in a very long time.

Sam's thoughts were interrupted by a loud horn blaring behind him. He looked to see his buddies from the fire hall pulling up beside him in the pumper truck. "Hey, Sam! Who's your girlfriend?" Geoff laughed out loud.

"She's no dammed friend of mine! I don't know who the hell she is, but she has no idea who she's dealing with!" Sam was frustrated.

"Hey Sam! I heard Trish left ya buddy! I wouldn't worry about it though, she was too hot for you anyway!" laughed John.

"Stand down, Rookie!" cautioned Geoff. "So you comin' to training tomorrow, Sam? The Captain's doing some training on the new ladder truck in the morning and he wants all the rookies there and was absolutely clear he didn't care how long you've been a volunteer. So you had better show up or you won't get certified."

Turning back and watching the Mustang driving away in the distance, Sam replied, "Yeah Geoff, I'll be there!"

Starting to pull away Geoff stopped, looked back out the window and yelled, "Hey Sam! John here says that you should put some bumper pads on that truck of yours in case your new girlfriend decides to come back into town."

Sam could hear Geoff and John laughing as they drove away.

"Yeah, yeah, get your laughs in now, boys!" Sam said to himself as he ran his hand through his hair. "You know...I wish there were just a few secrets in this town!" Grumbling he picked his hat up off the road slapped it against his leg to knock off the dust and placed it back on his head.

Yanking the door of his truck open Sam hopped in. "Aww for chrissakes!" The only way he could drive was to steer with his right hand and use his left to hold the door closed. *God dammit!* Still frustrated he headed to Old Bill's.

CHAPTER THREE

♡ ♡ ♡

Old Bill and Sam's dad, Jeb, opened up a mechanics shop in the 1970's when they were twenty-one years old and eager to start a business. As a kid, Sam always enjoyed sitting there after school each day while his dad and Bill worked on cars. Bill commented over the years that Sam was like the son he never had. After his father died, Sam felt lost and it was Bill who point blank told him to straighten up.

"Stop wallowing in grief and feeling sorry fer yerself Sam," he had said. "Get on with yer life and become a goddamn firefighter like ya always wanted. It's a bloody admirable profession. Yer dad may not have wanted that, but yer dad's not here now, and besides, as much as I loved him, yer dad could be an asshole at times." Sam had laughed because that comment pretty much summed up the friendship between his dad and Bill, but he was sure to heed Bill's message.

When Sam pulled up to the garage, Bill was walking out of one of the car bays, wiping his greasy hands with a cloth. Grabbing a coffee from the young Taylor kid who worked there Bill then growled at him to get back to work. The kid ran back into the shop and Bill laughed as he watched the kid trip over a hose, catching himself before he fell.

Sam chuckled when he thought about the Taylor boy trying to break into Bill's shop a few weeks back planning to steal tools to sell for cash. The kid, not expecting Bill would still be working at midnight, snuck through one of the shop windows and jumped to the floor only to come face to face with old man Walters himself.

"Thar ain't no runny-nosed little shit gonna steal from me as long as I'm alive and kickin' Will Taylor!" Bill assured the kid with a roar. As the story went, the kid was appropriately terrified. Once old man Walters notified the kid's parents and since his dad, Marty Taylor, was a local policeman, the kid got more than an 'ass-whoopin' and had to do some community service after school everyday working at Bill's shop for six months. Bill laughed until he cried when he was told about that one.

"Don't you think you're being a little tough on the kid, Bill?" Sam asked as he walked up and shook the older man's hand.

"Naw, Sam. He's a good kid but I'm not as young as I used ta be and I need ta keep the young'uns thinkin' I can still kick thar sorry asses from here ta the other end of town."

"But you CAN kick their asses, Bill," Sam added looking just in time to see Will tugging at a stuck oil pan plug in a customer's truck. When the kid finally tugged it free, oil spewed out all over his clothes and face. He muttered some expletive, threw the plug down and headed to the sink to clean up. Old Bill roared laughing and Sam had to admit, it looked good on the kid after trying to rob the old man. *Payback's a bitch kid!* Sam thought to himself.

Turning to Bill, Sam said, "I need my truck fixed, Bill."

Leaning in for a closer look at the damage, Bill asked, "What the hell happened ta 'er? It looks like she had the shit kicked out of 'er!"

Sam frowned and replied, "Yeah it did. Some bloody woman decided to make a U-turn in the middle of the road and hit me. Are you able to fix it this week, Bill?"

"More like a few weeks, Sam. Don't worry though, she looks like shit now but when I'm done with 'er she'll look like a beauty queen again!"

Tossing the greasy cloth down onto the bench Bill headed back to the garage shouting, "Gotta get back ta work, Sam. I need ta see if the kid has managed ta git himself cleaned up and back ta work. These kids today, Sam...ya always need ta keep thar sorry asses movin' or they'll git bored real quick and try ta rob ya blind!" That last part was said loud enough for the kid to hear as Bill walked into the shop laughing.

CHAPTER THREE

"Just leave her at the side, Sam, and grab yerself one of my rentals at no cost, the keys are in them. I'll be in touch."

Standing, staring at the so-called rentals Bill referred to, none of them were much to look at; they were all at least ten years old, dusty from lack of use and not one of them had power locks or windows. They all seemed to moan in defiance as Sam tried each one to see which may possibly last a few weeks until he got his truck back. The lucky winner was a 1990 four-door Ford Taurus that was dull red, gray cloth interior and looked like something your grandmother would drive. That said, it was clean inside and it only sounded somewhat like a tank but was still a far cry from his brand new GMC Sierra pick-up truck that had power everything. Sam sighed forlornly as he pulled out onto Main Street and sputtered towards home. He felt like a kid borrowing his dad's car, it was humiliating.

FOUR

Later that day, after settling into her new house, Sarah headed over to her sister Terri's for dinner. Her sister and brother-in-law A.J. lived in town on one of the quaintest streets Sarah had ever seen just a few doors down from the fire hall. Looking up, Sarah noticed the flag with the fire department logo flapping in the wind and the large siren attached to the outside of the building. *How they don't wake up at night when that siren blares for a call is beyond me*, thought Sarah.

Pulling into the driveway and getting out of her car, Sarah smiled. Terri seemingly had it all; a wonderful loving husband, a successful job, and a home that looked like it was out of House Monthly magazine; it was all so perfect. *I envy Terri. Her life is settled and mine is...well, who knows what mine is!* Sarah wasn't jealous though; she loved her sister and wanted nothing but the best for her. Before Sarah could even reach the front door it opened to a familiar face.

"Sarah! Sweetheart! How are you?"

Sarah loved A.J. He could do no wrong in her view and more importantly, he adored Terri, and she him. They were the perfect couple as far as Sarah was concerned.

"A.J.! It's so good to see you! Boy, have I missed you and your hugs!" Sarah said as A.J. released her from one of his famous bear hugs.

A.J. was six foot three, 225 pounds, built like a wrestler and someone most people wouldn't want to meet in a dark alley.

"Sarah, you haven't changed a bit. You look as beautiful as ever!"

"Aw, now stop that A.J., you're making me blush!" she laughed. A.J. was the local police chief but to Sarah he was just a big ole softie. "Listen, I parked around the side of the house is that okay or should I have parked on the road in front?"

"That's fine Sarah, most people park out front on the street because its closer to the front door but you're fine where you are." A.J. replied.

"Okay, so where is that amazing wife of yours?" Sarah could hardly wait to see her sister and tell her how much she loved her new home.

"She's in the kitchen working on dinner. Why don't you go on in to see her and I'll get you a drink. What are you drinking these days?" Sarah cringed at the thought of alcohol after her night out the week prior with Chloe drinking her Travis woes away and replied, "I think I'll just have a lemonade A.J., thanks," and with that she left to find her sister.

As A.J. had promised, Sarah found Terri in the kitchen making her famous spaghetti sauce. She had an apron on, her hair tied back, with sauce splattered all over her face and apron not to mention the mess on the stove, wall and counter.

"What the heck are you doing girl?" Sarah laughed as she walked in and gave her sister a hug and kiss on the cheek.

"Hi Sarah! I just turned the stove up for a minute while I made the garlic bread and when I turned around it was boiling and splattering all over the place." Terri fumed while trying to wipe up the mess.

CHAPTER FOUR

Sarah grabbed the cloth from her sister. "You go finish the garlic bread and whatever else you need to do. I'll clean this mess up." Looking to the ceiling Sarah laughed, "How the heck did you manage to have it splatter all the way up there? That must have been some trick!" Terri looked up, sighed and started laughing.

Just then A.J. came in with Sarah's lemonade, followed the girls' gaze to the ceiling and said, "I'm not even going to ask." He put down the lemonade and left the room chuckling. The girls laughed and finished getting dinner ready.

"Dinner was delicious as usual, Terri. I've missed your cooking." Sarah smiled contentedly after finishing dinner.

"By the way, Sarah, what the heck happened to the front of your car? I was outside and it looks like you were in an accident." A.J. inquired.

With disbelief, A.J. and Terri listened to Sarah's recount of the accident from earlier on that day.

"I know I shouldn't have left, A.J., but the guy was being so rude to me and I was tired." Sarah begged forgiveness.

A.J. frowned, "Well Sarah, it's true you shouldn't have left the scene of an accident. Technically you could be charged for leaving, however, by what you've told me how he was ranting and for safety reasons alone, I don't blame you for leaving. Who knows what he would have done if you stayed. If you give me his name or plate number, I can run it through the system so we can contact him and get things settled. It's better not to wait for him to contact you. Besides, you gave him your address..." Pausing he gave Sarah a stern look. "...and I certainly wouldn't want some unknown coming to your place to deal with this.

I would rather be there with you and be sure this gets dealt with in a reasonable manner."

Sarah could see the concern on his face and reluctantly added that she didn't have his name or his plate number, that she had left before getting it but could describe him if necessary. A.J. frowned and asked if she could describe the vehicle. Just then the doorbell rang and A.J. went to answer it.

"Oh Sarah, I have something I want to show you." Terri headed upstairs shouting to Sarah that she would be back in a few minutes to help clean up.

Starting to load the dishwasher Sarah's attention was soon drawn to the front hall. *I wonder what's going on.* She could hear the muffled voices but couldn't make out the conversation. *Whoever this guy is, he doesn't sound happy,* thought Sarah but didn't go to see what was going on, speculating that it was likely work related and A.J. needed some privacy. As the stranger's voice became louder Sarah wondered if she should go check after all to make sure everything was okay but then she heard A.J. roar with laughter followed by an angry response from the stranger. *Boy, I wish I could hear what they were saying.* Sarah's curiosity was starting to get the better of her. She heard the odd word, which wasn't much help, like 'took off', 'arrest' and 'completely unreasonable' but nothing fully audible.

Sarah could tell that A.J. thought something was hysterical. However, she could tell that the stranger was really upset. She could hear A.J. say something to the stranger, followed by silence then she could barely hear, "What the hell are you laughing about, A.J.?" The stranger definitely was not happy but A.J. couldn't stop laughing, in fact, he was practically crying he was laughing so hard.

Propping the kitchen door slightly open, Sarah then heard loud and clear, "It isn't funny A.J. She goddamned well smashed into my brand new truck! She should be charged with leaving the scene!" Sarah stopped dead in her tracks. *No way! It couldn't be!*

Storming out of the kitchen and down the hall towards the front door Sarah stopped at the sight of him.

"YOU! What are YOU doing here?" Pointing her finger towards the stranger at the door.

FIVE

THE STRANGER'S MOUTH DROPPED OPEN SEEING Sarah. He was so stunned at the sight of her that he never stopped to wonder why she was even at A.J.'s house to begin with.

By now Terri had made her way back downstairs and having heard the commotion wondered what was going on. "Hi Sam!" But seeing that he was upset asked, "What's wrong?"

"I don't know who you think you are but you have some nerve coming to my sister's home just to air your petty little problems!" Sarah insisted.

Confused, Terri demanded, "What the heck is going on?"

Glaring at A.J. who was still laughing, Sam then looked from Terri to Sarah and back again. Finally able to speak he asked, "She's your sister?"

"Yes, this is my sister, Sarah. Do you two know each other?" Terri was getting more confused by the minute.

"Terri, are you and A.J. friends with him?" By now, Sarah was also confused and starting to feel a little uncomfortable with the situation. She had been enjoying her relaxing evening until Mr. Gorgeous walked in and ruined it.

"Sam and A.J. have been friends since childhood but how do you two know each other?" Terri asked.

"This is the guy who was so rude to me today!" Sarah answered.

Retaliating, Sam said, "Listen lady! You hit my truck and left," then turning to A.J., demanded, "She should be arrested A.J. Now are you going to do it or what?"

Sarah's mouth dropped open. "Are you kidding me? You really want to have me arrested? You're out of your mind! My car was damaged too you know!"

Sam glared at her but remained silent. By now A.J. was settling down and asked Sam if he would like to come in for a drink to settle things before they got any worse. Both Sarah and Sam were hesitant. Sarah wanted him to leave and Sam wanted to give her a piece of his mind but thought he should curb his temper now that he knew she was Terri's sister and besides, A.J. wouldn't allow it. He was fiercely protective of his family, always had been, and Sam knew when to draw the line. *How could they be sisters? They look nothing alike. Terri is so sweet and reasonable while this one is so, outspoken, unreasonable, and a raving lunatic.*

"Come on, Sam, what do you say?" A.J. encouraged. Then putting his strong arm around his sister-in-law's shoulder said, "Sarah, remember what I said earlier," then gave her a sideways hug.

"Oh all right," Sarah begrudgingly agreed.

Reluctantly, Sam replied, "Okay A.J., I'll stay, but only if you tell your sister-in-law to curb her temper and be rational".

"Rational! YOU are telling ME to be RATIONAL! You know what pal? You are one of the most irrational people I have ever met!" Sarah's temper flew again and A.J., his arm still around her, gripped Sarah's shoulder tighter and steered her into the living room whispering in her ear, "Sarah, you need to calm down and take the time to get this sorted out. So just relax and I will help mediate things. Okay?" With that he went to the bar to pour some much-needed drinks for everyone.

Sarah sat down on the couch with her back to the front hall and could overhear Sam say, "Terri I can't believe you two are sisters. You are one of the most level-headed people I know and she's...well...she's NOT!"

Sarah's temper was starting to fume again until she heard Terri say, "Sam, Sarah's a darling girl. You just have to take the time to get to know her. She really is a wonderful person."

Sarah looked up as Terri and Sam came into the living room and sat down, Terri beside her sister and Sam in a chair across from them.

A.J., bringing a beer in for Sam and a glass of white wine each for Sarah and Terri, took his stance beside the couch near Sarah. Sarah smiled when she accepted the drink and looking at Sam said sarcastically, "At least someone here is a gentleman." Even though he knew he never would, Sam just wanted to slug her, *Just once*, he thought.

A.J. was still chuckling but managed to maintain his composure so they could work things out and move on. He knew this wasn't going to be easy because Sam was extremely stubborn and A.J. had also been witness to Sarah's temper in the past.

"Okay, so first of all, Sam, this is Terri's sister, Sarah, and Sarah, this is my best friend, Sam. I thought you two should be properly introduced since you have clearly already met," he said with a mischievous grin. Sarah and Sam just glared at each other from across the room. Silence.

Terri shifted uncomfortably in her seat and looked anxiously at A.J. who just silently mouthed to her that everything would be okay, and smiled. Terri nervously smiled, rolled her eyes and took a large gulp of her wine.

"Sam, I spoke to Sarah earlier about what happened and she has naturally agreed to pay for any damages to your truck." Sarah's face went blank. She had no interest in making nice with this guy but was going through the motions for the sake of A.J. and Terri. Sam said nothing allowing A.J. to continue.

"Since there is only one place in town that does body work, Sarah, it will be impossible for Sam to get more than one quote and you will have to pay whatever Bill charges."

Sarah just rolled her eyes and mumbled, "Yeah okay." Sam smirked and winked at her, which really irritated her. She responded with an ice-cold stare. *Where does he get the nerve?*

"Sam, I know Sarah shouldn't have taken off and you do have the right to have her charged for leaving the scene of an accident..."

Sarah stood up "What? Are you kidding me? He was practically threatening me! I left in self-defence! Who the hell does he think..." A.J. put his hand firmly on Sarah's shoulder and forcibly sat her back down on the couch.

"Sit down, Sarah! I never said you would be charged. Of course you won't be," A.J. glared at Sam who immediately lost the smirk off his face.

"Now Sam, I would suggest that you apologize to Sarah for the way you approached her at the scene of the accident..."

"What? Are you kidding me A.J.? There is no WAY I will apologize to her. For what? I didn't do anything wrong. It was your sister-in-law who made an illegal U-turn right into my truck and for chrissakes it was your sister-in-law who drove away without even so much as an apology for the damage she caused! Are you mad? ME apologize to HER?!" Sam was livid. *This is a friggin joke. I only stopped by to have a beer with A.J. Why the hell should I apologize to her? I just want my truck fixed and my money and I never want to see her again*, fumed Sam.

CHAPTER FIVE

"Oh for God's sake shuddup Sam and let me finish! You two are driving me crazy! Do you want my help or not? I could leave the room and have the two of you sort it out but I would be afraid you'd kill each other!" A.J. was now getting frustrated with the two of them.

Terri took another gulp of her wine, uncomfortably shifting in her seat.

"This is the bottom line. Sam you apologize to Sarah for what you said and how you acted today. Sarah you apologize for hitting Sam's truck, while making an illegal U-turn I might add, and when Sam gets the tab from Bill, you pay him in full and then the two of you never have to deal with each other again. Oh, and by the way, I'm not asking you to do this, I'm telling you or I'll throw you both in jail in the same cell until you do work it out!" A.J. had raised his voice at this point and was staring them both down to the point of making them both feel uncomfortable. He was met with silence once again.

"Now then, Terri and I are going into the kitchen to finish the dishes and put the coffee on and by the time we get back you two had better have made peace. Oh and by the way, Sam, Sarah, don't leave this room or I'll have you both arrested." A.J. gave them both a stern nod and turned to leave the room.

Terri quickly grabbed her drink and avoiding eye contact, tiptoed past Sarah and Sam scurrying into the kitchen after A.J. She couldn't get out of there fast enough. For Terri this was the most uncomfortable few minutes of her life. *Why can't everyone just get along?* she thought.

Sam and Sarah sat in silence glaring at each other until Sam quietly said, "You look nothing like your sister." He was uncomfortable with making small talk.

"Yeah, well, Terri got all the looks in the family." Sarah still felt defensive.

Sam looked over at her as she nervously wrapped a piece of her hair around her index finger and thought to himself, *I wouldn't necessarily say that*, but aloud asked Sarah, "So what are we going to do about this business?" Sam really didn't want this conversation yet thought better of leaving (although it did cross his mind) because he knew A.J. wasn't kidding when he said he would throw them both in jail.

Sarah remained silent.

After a moment Sam offered, "Okay then. How about you just pay me for the damages and I won't have you charged with leaving the scene of an accident," he offered up arrogantly.

"What? Are you kidding me? You are such a jerk!"

Sam's anger was starting to brew again. "Listen lady! Why don't you just admit it was a stupid thing to do, pay me my money and we never have to see each other again?" Sam's voice was getting louder.

"You know, guys like you always seem to think you can get what you want by being pushy! Well, I'm not going to put up with that! Why don't you just apologize to me for the way you acted and we can move on." Sarah was having a difficult time controlling her temper.

"Why the hell should I apologize? You are the one who stupidly made the U-turn into my truck, then drove away. If anyone should be apologizing it should be you."

"Unbelievable! How dare you call me stupid!" Sarah stood up and glared at Sam. "I have no intention of apologizing to you!"

"Lady, it's a good thing you're A.J.'s sister-in-law or I wouldn't be so understanding." Sam was shocked at how belligerent she was.

"Understanding! You call this understanding?" Sarah shook her head in utter disbelief.

"I sure do! If it wasn't for A.J., I'd be having you arrested right now!" Sam shot back.

CHAPTER FIVE

"You can't be serious! Oh my God!" Sarah wasn't sure how they were going to resolve their differences but it didn't seem like it would be happening anytime soon.

Walking over to pour herself another glass of wine Sarah didn't realize that Sam had followed behind her. Turning around, she slammed into him spilling the entire contents of her drink down the front of him. Gasping, she took a step back. Seeing Sam with his mouth dropped open and his shirt soaked with wine, she wasn't sure how he was going to react but couldn't stop herself from laughing aloud at the sight of him.

Sam was less than impressed. "What the…?" Looking up at Sarah he asked, "You think this is funny? You are a walking disaster lady! Everytime I'm near you something happens to me for chrissakes!" Sarah couldn't stop laughing even though Sam was so irritated.

♡ ♡ ♡

A.J. and Terri figured it wasn't a good sign when they heard Sam and Sarah yelling at each other and stayed in the kitchen. Once they heard laughter they figured it was safe to go back but were surprised to see Sam soaking wet and Sarah holding an empty glass and laughing.

"Oh my God, Sarah, you didn't need to throw your drink on Sam!" Terri ran to get a dry shirt for him to change into.

A.J. started laughing which irritated Sam even more. "You know A.J., you could be a little more sympathetic." Sam glared at his friend.

Sarah was trying to regain her composure. "I didn't throw my drink on him A.J., he walked into it, honest!"

"She's a train wreck, A.J. Seriously, no one is safe around her! At least I know I'm not!" Sam's anger was waning and he found himself grinning.

Terri returned with a towel and a shirt for Sam. She was still annoyed at Sarah for throwing her drink at him. "You know, Sarah, you really must learn to control your temper," Terri scolded her.

A.J. came to Sarah's defence, "Relax Hon, it was an accident. It's all good." Terri handed Sam a towel to dry off and then passed him the shirt to change into.

"So can I assume you two can work things out?" A.J. asked. Looking at one another, Sam and Sarah both conceded that they could.

"Listen, I shouldn't have behaved the way I did. It was uncalled for." Sam offered.

"Well, I suppose I wasn't any better, Sam. Once you find out, let me know what I owe you for the damages and I'll get a cheque to you right away," said Sarah.

"Okay so who's up for another drink?" A.J. asked.

The foursome spent the next couple of hours talking and laughing and the more Sarah got to know Sam the more she liked him. *Okay, Mr. Gorgeous is working his way back up the scales again to an eight out of ten*, Sarah thought watching him as he spoke to A.J. about the break up with his girlfriend and how he was looking forward to some training at work.

"Well, I'm outta here. I need to be at the fire hall tomorrow morning for training and Spud won't be happy if I show up late." Sam chuckled.

"Who's Spud?" Sarah asked.

CHAPTER FIVE

"Captain Reginald Turcotte, Reg for short, or at the fire hall, Spud. He loves potatoes so much that it landed him the nickname Spud way back when he was a rookie and it has stuck ever since. I can assure you that Spud doesn't put up with being late, so we'll talk later A.J."

Giving Terri a big hug Sam said, "Terri, once again it was a pleasure and you know that if you ever get tired of this guy I'm here for the taking! He doesn't deserve you, you know." Sam gave Terri a kiss on the cheek before letting her go.

Turning to Sarah, Sam said, "Well Sarah, what can I say? It wasn't a pleasure meeting you at first but it certainly has been tonight. Take care and we'll be in touch soon."

Sam walked over and shook Sarah's hand, then, turning to shake A.J.'s, tripped over Sarah's purse falling forward into A.J., which sent them both back into the chair that A.J. had been sitting in. The chair then tipped backwards sending them both onto the floor, chair and all, one on top of the other.

Picking himself up off the floor and reaching a hand out to help his friend, Sam lamented, "For chrissakes, A.J., would you please do something about your sister-in-law before she kills someone!" Sarah and Terri laughed at the sight before them.

After leaving the house, Sam thought how much he actually liked Sarah. *She's an accident waiting to happen, that one. I wonder if any of her boyfriends have survived their relationship*, he chuckled to himself.

Sarah left her sister's place shortly after Sam with a big smile on her face. *Mr. Gorgeous wasn't half bad after all. Too bad I'm staying away from men for a while*, she thought as she got into her car to head home. Before she was able to start the car her cell phone rang and seeing it was Travis, decided to answer it with the intention of telling him to stop calling her. Travis immediately began talking, "So Sweetheart, did you enjoy your evening with Terri and A.J.? Who's your new boyfriend?"

Sarah was a little uneasy. *Is he spying on me?* she wondered looking around to see if she could catch sight of him.

"Sarah honey, it's no longer just about the car. I want you back baby and I won't put up with you seeing someone else." Travis sounded drunk which concerned Sarah because he could be mean when he was drunk and she wasn't quite sure how to respond.

"Baby? Are you there? You ruined my car and now you're seeing someone else. Understand I can't let you get away with that. Do you hear me, Sarah?" His tone growing angrier, "I WON'T let you get away with it."

Sarah was getting scared and hung up the phone. She sat in her car unsure of what to do next. She could tell A.J. but she didn't want to get him involved. This was her problem and he had already been dragged into her issue with Sam, which was enough.

Sarah fully expected Travis to call back but he didn't. *How had he known I was with A.J. and Terri? How did he even know about Sam?* She always knew that Travis was a bit unstable when he was drunk but never thought he would stoop to these levels to frighten her. Starting her car she headed home deep in thought. *I think I know Travis well enough to know he would never do anything to harm me. He's just trying to scare me and it's not going to work.* Putting Travis out of her mind, Sarah reflected back on her evening and how much she had enjoyed getting to know Sam a bit better.

The next morning Sam uncharacteristically overslept and arrived late to the fire hall for training. To say Captain Turcotte wasn't happy would have been an understatement.

"Where the hell have you been, Ward? For chrissakes, you were told to be here at 0700 hours SHARP!! Not 0710! The volunteers may have been okay with your tardiness but you're full-time now and I can tell you that I'm not putting up with any of your sorry ass late shit! Now get your gear on and get the hell on that truck! You're holding the whole crew up because you don't know how the hell to be on time, you selfish son-of-a-bitch!! Now move it!!"

What got his goat this morning? He seems more miserable than usual, thought Sam who knew enough not to mess with Spud on a good day let alone a bad one. Saying nothing, Sam ran to get his gear.

Goddamn rookies! They'll learn how to be on time if they are going to work on my crew, thought Reg. He was in a particularly foul mood this morning and knew it. *These rookies had better work their asses off today or there will be hell to pay,* he thought. Even though he was mad as hell, Reg found it rather amusing to watch the likes of Ward tripping and falling over his turnout gear as he scrambled to put it on while running to get on the fire truck. *Goddamn it feels good to scare the shit out of them.* Reg smiled as he took another sip of his coffee. *I'm starting to feel better now.*

"Get your ass on that truck, Ward! We have a training ground to get to. Move it!" Reg yelled. Once Sam was on board, Reg hopped into the front passenger's seat and signalled the driver to get moving.

In the back of the truck, Geoff turned to Sam and said, "Holy shit Sam, what the fuck's wrong with you? I told you to have your ass here by 0700 didn't I?"

"Yeah, yeah, Geoff, shut the hell up!" Sam was irritated and in no mood for a lecture from Geoff.

Reg chuckled to himself as he overheard their conversation behind him. He knew Sam was as good a person and firefighter as they came but he also knew that he couldn't be soft on him because his life would be on the line one day and he needed to be prepared, they all did. Yup, whenever Reg trained new recruits, he laid it out on the line and told them "If you can't take the heat then get the hell out of my fire hall boys because I don't want some runny-nosed, whiny assholes working on my crew!"

SEVEN

That same morning Sarah was up bright and early. It was another warm day for September. The day was sunny with clear blue skies, absolute perfection in her opinion. Grabbing a cup of coffee she walked down to the shoreline and sat at the end of the dock with her feet dangling in the cool, clear water. She took a deep breath of the fresh air and closing her eyes listened to the sounds of the lake. It was so peaceful and calm which was exactly what she needed after the last couple of eventful days. The sun on her face was a welcome balance to the coolness of the morning. In the distance, a loon echoed. The breeze gently rustling the leaves practically put her into a trance and gave her a moment of sanctuary that she had not experienced in a long time. Taking in a deep, slow breath Sarah knew that she would love it here. There was peace and tranquility – she was relaxed. Opening her eyes she enjoyed looking at the water sparkling in the sunlight, the loon gently dipping into the water only to reappear yards away and the waves slowly lapping against the shoreline. Yes, this was home now and Sarah couldn't be happier. *It's hard to believe that only yesterday morning I was still in Watertown with Travis, that cheating bastard.* She could feel herself tensing up just at the thought of him and decided to shake it off and focus on moving on.

Heading back to the house she was reluctant to start unpacking. The remainder of her belongings weren't due to arrive until the next day and she really just wanted some down-time to recoup from these last few weeks and from what she would describe as an emotional rollercoaster. Seeing that she had a phone message Sarah listened to it and was happy to hear it was from her dad.

"Hey Kiddo, it's Dad. Your mother and I have decided to come and help you settle into your new place. We plan on coming Friday and staying for a couple of weeks. Now listen, we don't want any arguments. We are coming and that's final! We'll talk to you before we leave, and by the way, we plan on bringing all of those boxes of yours that have been in the garage for years. It's about time you go through them, they are taking up too much space and I want them out of here. Bye Kiddo. What? Karen, I can't hear you, what did you say? Oh for God's sake, Karen, yes, she needs to take those boxes, I have no room in the garage for the car... yes she does…anyway, Kiddo, see you soon." And with that Sarah's dad hung up the phone.

Typical Mom and Dad, Sarah chuckled to herself. She was looking forward to them coming and helping her get organized. It was overwhelming because the house needed some work and she wasn't all that handy with tools but her father was. She smiled. *This day is getting better all the time.*

Thinking about Travis again, the smile left her face. Remembering how upset he had been about his car made her very happy at the time but she also knew that she shouldn't have lost her temper the way she did. Sarah was known for being short-tempered and her mother often scolded her for being so unreasonable. *I'm not that unreasonable. Mom just doesn't like confrontation. Neither does Terri for that matter. I'd say Dad and I are the most alike when it comes to dealing with difficult situations.*

Reflecting back to a couple of weeks prior Sarah couldn't help but smile at the thought of her father's reaction when she told him what happened with Travis. *Boy, Travis is lucky Dad hasn't gotten a hold of him,* Sarah chuckled as she thought back to that day.

CHAPTER SEVEN

♡ ♡ ♡

"That son-of-a-bitch, I'm gonna kill him!" George Roberts was livid. "He hurt my little girl and there is gonna be hell to pay!" Sarah cringed. Her father was yelling so loudly she had to hold the phone away from her ear.

"Where's he at right now, Sarah? I want to have words with that boy!" And by words, Sarah knew he wanted to punch Travis out. She also knew well enough not to have her father and Travis in the same city together let alone the same building.

"Now Dad." she offered cautiously.

"Well, where the hell is he?" George bellowed into the phone.

"George, please! This is something Sarah can work out. I'm sure you don't have to get involved, dear." Sarah could hear her mother in the background trying to reason with her father.

"Karen, I'm already involved! That son-of-a-bitch hurt our baby girl and by God he's gonna hear from me about it," George responded but Sarah wished it wasn't quite so loud because her ear was starting to hurt.

"But George, we should stay out of it. We need to let Sarah deal with it and if she needs help, she knows to call us. She's a big girl now. Honestly, George, you overreact to everything. You need to calm down." *That's an understatement and clearly ironic coming from Mom,* thought Sarah, knowing her mother often overreacted to things.

Sarah knew her mom was desperately trying to be the voice of reason without luck. She also knew her dad would never calm down when it came to one of his two daughters being hurt. Her mother told her after the fact, "Admittedly, I would have loved to let Daddy punch out Travis, dear, because I never did like him, however, I didn't dare voice that opinion or your father would have taken that as permission to go and do just that."

"Karen, I'm gonna punch the shit out of that kid and if he ever goes near my little girl again, I'll have A.J. arrest him and throw his sorry ass in jail!" *Interesting,* Sarah thought, *considering A.J. and Travis are in two completely different cities.*

"Dad?" Sarah wanted to stop the three-way conversation but knew she wasn't likely being heard from the other end of the phone.

"George, really, you need to calm down!" Karen responded. *This is true,* Sarah agreed.

"I AM calm, Karen!" George yelled. *Definitely not true,* Sarah smiled.

"Dad," she again tried to get her father's attention.

"And don't you tell me to calm down when our little girl's heart has been broken by that sorry ass, going nowhere, cheating, piece-of-shit football player!" *True again*, Sarah silently agreed once more.

"Dad!" Sarah called into the phone again with no response. "DAD!"

"What! I'm talking with your mother right now, Sarah. Don't interrupt!" George was annoyed.

"Dad, I'm fine, really! Well, I wasn't fine, but I'm fine now and if I think I need you to come down and punch out Travis then I'll call you. Seriously, Daddy, you should know by now that I can handle my own with men." Sarah was determined to keep talking before her father started up again and she couldn't finish.

"I'm going to deal with Travis so don't worry. He'll get the message loud and clear that there's no messing with one of George Roberts' girls!" Sarah hoped that her little speech would calm her father down enough to allow her to get off the phone.

CHAPTER SEVEN

After a moment of thought, George said, "Well, Kiddo, I guess I'll have to trust you on this one but don't you take any shit from him and you be sure that he understands loud and clear that there are no second chances when it comes to hurting my little girl!" George was starting to settle down.

Of his two daughters George knew that Sarah was the one that could handle herself. She always could, even as a young girl. There were many times that George and Karen would get called to Sarah's elementary school to speak with the principal about the fact that Sarah had once again wrestled some boy to the ground because he had made some derogatory comment to her. The boy and Sarah would argue it out until she decided she didn't like the direction the argument was going and then she would tackle the boy to the ground and sit on him. George chuckled at the thought. *She was his daughter all right!* He smiled and reminded himself that yes, his youngest daughter was no one to mess with.

"Don't worry, Daddy, I'm not done with Travis yet!" Sarah smiled at the thought. She hadn't figured out quite what her revenge would be but once she did then ole Travis had better watch out!

When the day finally arrived and Sarah left Travis, she called her dad on the way to Forestville to tell him about the 'note' she left Travis.

George roared with laughter. "Kiddo, you make me proud! That was brilliant! But you know he could make you pay for the damages...but hell, I'll even pay for them because it'll be worth every penny just knowing that son-of-a-bitch got payback!"

Thinking back to that conversation, Sarah smiled. Her dad loved a good fight and when it came to one of his daughter's getting hurt, he didn't care if it was a clean fight or not. He just loved payback!

Shaking herself back to the 'here and now' Sarah remembered she had no food in the house to even cook a proper meal for herself, let alone her parents and quickly showered to head into town.

Hopping into her car she was reminded that she had better go to the body shop and find out how much it would cost to get it fixed. The damage didn't seem all that extensive but it was bad enough that her hood wouldn't close properly and she needed to bungee cord it shut.

EIGHT

The grocery store wasn't busy and Sarah managed to get everything she needed quickly, not to mention learning from the little old lady in front of her in the checkout line that the best hair stylist in town was named Cathy. Apparently Cathy worked out of the barbershop but Sarah shouldn't go there on a Monday because it was Cathy's day off. On the other hand, Fred the Barber was as good a hair cutter as Cathy ever was but he was having an affair with Wendy, who lived on Stone Hill Lane. *Not sure what that has to do with his hair cutting abilities.* Sarah chuckled to herself.

Apparently, Cathy had told Fred that Wendy's husband Bernie would find out one day and then Fred had better run because Bernie was a hunter and wouldn't hesitate to shoot Fred if he found out about Wendy and Fred having an affair.

"...and you know, dear, Fred just doesn't seem to care that ole Bernie could shoot him dead because Bernie is Tom's son-in-law and Tom gets Fred to cut his hair and Fred says that Tom can't stand Bernie anyway and would be more than happy if Wendy and Bernie D-I-V-O-R-C-E-D". She spelled the word slowly while whispering into Sarah's ear so no one else could hear, although she was speaking so loudly the entire store could hear her quite clearly. *If only she turned up her own hearing aid*, Sarah thought with a smile. *Then she would hear what everyone else was hearing.*

"It's absolutely scandalous!" She finished off with a firm nod of her head just as she reached the cashier.

Oh my God, my head is spinning. Sarah was dumbfounded. *There really are no secrets in a small town,* she thought. As the little old lady left the store she waved good-bye to Sarah and off she went. Sarah chuckled to herself; *Fred had better hope Bernie never comes grocery shopping at the same time as that lady.*

Loading groceries into her car, Sarah noticed the garage across the road and decided to head over. Pulling up in front, she got out and saw that it was a two-bay garage with currently only one small car on a hoist and an older gentleman working underneath it. The man looked to be about her dad's age, with a full head of grey hair, maybe six feet tall and a slim build. His face and hands were dirty from grease and when he saw Sarah, he smiled warmly, wiped his hands with a cloth and walked out to meet her.

"Good afternoon young lady! My name is Bill Walters, Old Bill the folks around here call me. What can I do fer yer?" Sarah immediately liked him. He was very friendly and sweet with a kind face.

"Good afternoon, Mr. Walters! My name is Sarah Roberts. I was wondering if you would be able to take a look at the damage on my car to see if you could fix it for me and let me know what it might cost."

Sarah went to shake old Bill's hand but he showed her the grease on them and said, "I don't think yer want ta shake my hand, lovely lady, but I would be more than happy ta take a look at yer car fer yer."

Sarah led the way. Taking a close look Bill asked, "What happened ta her? Did yer hit someone or did they hit yer?" Bill knelt down to inspect the grill and broken headlight more closely.

CHAPTER EIGHT

"Well, I actually hit someone and now I have to pay for their damages as well as mine. But quite honestly, I don't want to put it through insurance because I think it will put my rates through the roof. Do you think it's something you can fix Mr. Walters?" Sarah asked hopefully.

"Now listen, young lady, if we're goin' ta git along, yer just goin' ta have ta call me Old Bill or Bill but yer certainly can't call me Mr. Walters. That was my father's name!"

Sarah laughed, "Okay then, Bill it is!"

"I must admit this is the week fer body repairs. I have another job ta do over the next few weeks but I could certainly take yer car after that. Let me just git a hammer and bang the dents out as best I can so yer can at least shut yer hood without having ta use a bungee cord."

And with that Bill disappeared into his shop and returned a few minutes later carrying said hammer. After some loud banging around on the hood, in no time at all Bill had managed to get it to close on its own again.

"Now yer just goin' ta have ta be careful driving at night with just one headlight, Miss, because I can't do anything about the damaged one until I git the body work fixed up first. As far as a price fer fixing up yer car, well I can't give you that until I actually git working on it but I'm guessing around two thousand bucks."

"Well thank you so much, Bill. I appreciate you taking the time to fix my hood so it will at least close on its own. Now what do I owe you for this?" Sarah was grateful that her hood was semi-functional again.

"Don't worry about it, my dear. Let's just say I'm grateful ta have had a visit from such a lovely young lady taday. Just leave me with yer phone number and I will call yer when I'm ready ta work on yer car." Old Bill liked Sarah and wondered why he had never seen her around town before.

"That's great Bill, thank you!" Sarah wrote her phone number down. She then remembered that she also wanted to speak to him about Sam's truck and what the cost would be to fix it.

Once Bill realized that it was Sarah who had hit Sam, he roared with laughter. "Well yer sure managed ta git under that boy's skin Miss Sarah! And I can assure ya, he's not used ta anyone putting him in his place." Letting out a belly laugh, Bill added, "But no worries, I can fix both vehicles up ta look as good as new and I'll be sure ta cut yer a good deal. Don't let ole Sam scare yer. He's a big ole teddy bear inside. I should know, I've known him since he was a young lad. A more reliable person yer won't find and believe me, yer can trust him like no other."

After getting some insight into Sam from Bill, as well as a rough estimate of cost for repairing Sam's truck, Sarah said good-bye and headed back home to put away the groceries.

NINE

THE FIRE TRUCK PULLED INTO the station at the end of a long training session and Sam couldn't have been happier. Turcotte had been particularly hard on them and Sam knew enough not to complain or his life would have been significantly harder. Wiping sweat from his forehead with the back of his forearm, Sam hopped down off the truck and headed over to hang up his bunker gear. Geoff had already hung his jacket and was taking his boots off when he looked up at Sam and said, "Thanks again for being late this morning, Sam. You fucking well handed Spud an invitation to work the shit out of us today. Maybe next time you could consider setting an alarm clock."

"What the hell are you complaining about? I'm the one who's ass he rode all day long." Sam was frustrated with the way the day went. Nothing went right and he constantly made stupid mistakes. It wasn't like he didn't know what he was doing but it didn't seem to matter what he did, Spud managed to find fault in it and made him do it over just one more time. Taking off his bunker gear, Sam was exhausted from the day and couldn't wait to get to the pub and grab a cold one.

"Ward! Where the hell do you think you're going, Rookie?" Captain Turcotte yelled from across the truck bay.

"Just hanging up my bunker gear, Captain." Sam had to stop himself from adding, 'What the fuck does it matter to you'.

"Well tonight you're washing the truck all by yourself and making damn sure it's squeaky clean before you leave today. I figure the rest of the boys deserve a break. It's the least you can do after being late this morning and holding the whole crew up. So get at it, Rookie!" And with that, Captain Turcotte left the truck bay and headed to the Captain's office.

Sam was tired and fed up but knew enough to keep his mouth shut. The rookie always got dumped on and the more they complained the more work they got. Everyone had his or her turn as rookie and it was Sam's turn now regardless of how many years he'd volunteered. Once you became full-time you were a rookie and your volunteer time didn't enter into the picture. At the fire hall you learned to let things roll off your back pretty quickly. If you didn't you would never fit in.

"Hey Sam! Looks good on ya' buddy. I'll have a cold one for you at the pub but if you hurry up I still might be there to buy you one." Geoff couldn't resist giving Sam a hard time. Sam had to give him that though because Geoff had been the rookie for so long he was just happy to have someone else be the focus for a change.

"Yeah you do that," Sam flipped Geoff his middle finger then watched him turn and head out the door laughing.

By the time Sam arrived at the Old Beagle pub he saw that most of the guys had already left for home but Geoff and Rudy were still there with John, another rookie.

"Hey Sam, glad you could make it!" Geoff smirked.

CHAPTER NINE

"Dam truck was caked in mud and took a while to clean. Could Spud not have gone along Route 16 then up Highway 48 and across Donway Flats to the training grounds? At least all those roads are paved. It's like he took all the dirt roads on purpose." Sam ordered a beer on tap from the waitress and an order of chicken wings.

"Spud said that Highway 48 was under construction or something like that. I haven't driven up there in so long I wouldn't know." Rudy took a final drink of his beer and banging his empty glass on the table threw down twenty dollars to pay.

"Well boys, I'm outta here. Deb is cooking steaks on the BBQ tonight and I'm not about to miss that. She can't really cook worth a damn but by God she sure can BBQ and her marinated steaks are some of the best I've ever eaten. See you tomorrow and let's hope Spud's in a better frame of mind."

Standing and grabbing his car keys off the table, Rudy asked, "Hey, Sam, John, when's your start date as full-time? I thought next week was going to be your first official week?"

"Naw, Spud hasn't assigned permanent shifts or trucks yet. Apparently, that's happening for all rookies the end of next week once training wraps up," Sam offered.

"It can't come soon enough for me," John added.

Picking up his beer Sam toasted, "Well boys! Here's to us and here's hoping Spud won't be a miserable son-of-a-bitch tomorrow!" Everyone laughed and then Rudy was off.

"So Sam, what's happening with your truck? Is Old Bill able to fix it?" Geoff asked.

"And hey, who's your new girlfriend?" John laughed.

"Well, that's a whole other ballgame. That girl who hit my truck?"

"Yeah, I remember. The one who left you in her dust as she drove away." Geoff goaded.

Geoff was unfazed as Sam glared at him. "It turns out that she's A.J.'s sister-in-law. Christ! Can you believe that?" Sam updated them on the events of the night before at A.J.'s and of course, they laughed at Sam's expense. Sam was not amused but didn't let it show.

"Are you kidding? So how much is it going to cost Old Bill to fix it and I hope to hell you are going to make her pay to have it repaired." John added.

"You can count on it but I have to back off a bit. If I give her too much of a hard time A.J. will kill me but man that girl is an accident waiting to happen. If it's going to happen it will happen to everyone else around her but not her." Sam shook his head in disbelief.

The waitress brought his wings and he dug in. He was starving after the hard day he had. He was happy training was almost over. In less than two weeks his full-time career was starting and he couldn't wait. This had been a long time coming and a dream he almost didn't pursue but was glad he had. Firefighting had been a passion of his for a very long time and although the day hadn't been the easiest Sam still had no regrets.

TEN

FRIDAY ARRIVED QUICKLY AND SARAH knew her mom and dad would show up early in the day. *Dad always likes getting an early start and won't put up with Mom 'lollygagging' as he puts it.*

Sarah managed to get her guest room presentable so that her parents could at least settle in and have a proper place to sleep. Her furniture had arrived the day prior and although most of it was stockpiled throughout the house she managed to get a few key pieces like the couch and tables for the living room set up, at least temporarily, until she shifted everything into their permanent places. That's where her father would come in handy, helping her lift and move the heavier pieces and her mother's specialty was the finishing touches. Sarah was looking forward to seeing her parents. She missed them and hadn't seen them since before she split up with Travis and she hadn't realized how badly she needed some Mom and Dad time.

"Kiddo, we're here!" her father shouted from outside. "Karen, I said just leave that there and I'll get it later."

"But George, it's in the way, dear. We can barely get into the house." Sarah's mom sounded frustrated.

"Karen, I'm telling you to leave it and I'll get it later. Sarah, where are you? It's Mom and Dad."

"Daddy!" Sarah ran into her father's arms and was rewarded with an extra long hug.

"How are you, Kiddo? It's good to see you. Have you heard from that no good football player since we talked last?"

"Talk about getting straight to the point. No Daddy, I haven't." Sarah felt bad telling a little white lie but she didn't want him to worry.

"Good. Glad to hear it! If he calls while your mother and I are here I expect you to put him on the phone with me so I can tell him exactly how I feel about hurting my baby girl!"

"Daddy stop. Travis seems to be moving on with that tramp cheerleader Gretchen and anyway, I'm sure I will get a bill from him soon enough for the damages to his car. He was pretty mad." Sarah saw the look on her mother's face and added, "And I know I shouldn't have done it, Mom, but what's done is done and at the time it seemed like the thing to do."

"Sarah dear, you really must learn to control your temper!"

"Well I had considered shooting him in the leg so he couldn't play football for a while but didn't really like the thought of going to jail." Sarah uncomfortably laughed this comment off but stopped when she saw that her mother wasn't laughing.

Sarah appeased her mother by agreeing with her, then gave her mom a big hug and suggested she finish unpacking while Sarah made lunch.

After lunch, they sat in the sunroom, relaxing. It overlooked the lake and Sarah loved the view. The leaves were slowly starting to change colour and she imagined it would be spectacular once they were in full autumn colour.

Her parents took the time to catch her up on everything back in the old neighbourhood. She had moved away from home ten years ago and really missed all their old neighbours and friends. There always was an interesting group of people living there like Mrs. Carter, who had been their next-door neighbour for over twenty years. Mrs. Carter, or Flo, was an alcoholic but a harmless one and as much as Sarah's parents didn't agree with her drinking they left it in her husband's capable hands to try to cut her back. Problem was, if her husband Matt tried to reduce the alcohol in the drinks he made her, Flo would notice immediately and tell him to get back to the bar and try again. She didn't like anyone cheating her out of a good buzz. On the upside, Flo was full of laughs and when she was sober she was one of the most reliable individuals you could ever meet. If you needed her for anything she was there.

The neighbours on the other side were the Brown Family. Esther Brown was one of her mother's best friends and they did almost everything together. Esther was a minister at the local community church and the fact that Karen and George were Catholic and had no interest in converting had never been an issue. A few times a month the two couples got together to play euchre and that's when the fun began as far as Sarah was concerned. The arguments that would take place among the four of them were hilarious. Arguments like between Esther and her husband Bob, over who played the wrong card at the wrong time and George would question Karen as to why she didn't go alone when it was perfectly obvious she had a lone hand. Then every once in a while one person would accuse the other of cheating but in the end it was all in good fun and if things became too heated, Esther would stop the game to get food and drinks, which always seemed to simmer the group down. Sarah really did miss them.

Once her parents were settled in, Sarah showed them around her new home and property. It wasn't a surprise that her father's favourite place was the dock. They had a cottage growing up and she knew her dad missed it but Mom wasn't interested in spending every summer there alone, so they sold it a few years prior. Sarah was hoping her parents would buy a place in Forestville closer to her and Terri. Terri had talked to them about moving many times but they wanted to stay where they were for the time being. However, Sarah had noticed them softening recently and was hoping Terri could seal the deal during their visit.

Once the tour was over George wanted to get started on moving furniture into place and asked for a list of repairs that needed to be done so he could just work away at his own pace. This was where her father was happiest, puttering around the house.

Sarah chuckled when her dad turned on her kitchen taps only to discover the hot and cold were backwards.

"Good God, can no one do a proper job these days? Sarah hand me my toolbox would you? I'm going to fix this once and for all! Some contractors know shit and this was one of them obviously." Sarah just laughed and handed her father his toolbox.

Sarah found it heart-warming having her parents around to help her set up her new place and by dinnertime it was starting to feel like home.

ELEVEN

Come Saturday morning, Sam woke up regretting that he had to deal with Trish. The last thing he wanted was his ex-girlfriend coming back to the house to pick up her belongings. It had been a long hard week of training and he wasn't in the mood to deal with her. To say the least, it had been a rough ending to a rough relationship. He had unfortunately gone with cute, not smart and that hadn't paid off. At the beginning he thought it was endearing that she really wasn't the 'smartest cookie in the jar' and laughed it off. As time went by it became mildly annoying and then eventually downright embarrassing and he wondered how anyone could possibly be so stupid. The guys at the fire hall started calling her 'Trish the Dish' and spent all their waking hours reciting every dumb blond joke they could, even though Trish was, in fact, a red head. Not that he could blame them because she gave them enough ammunition to work with.

Sam still regretted the day she stopped by to visit him at work one night he was on stand-by and asked what phone number people should call if they wanted to reach the fire hall in an emergency. The guys told her that it was like every other emergency number and you would call 'nine', 'eleven'. Trish stood there for a few minutes and then asked, "But I don't understand. How is that possible?" Shaking his head Geoff offered, "Well, obviously they dial that number and call us!" The real problem arose when a puzzled Trish asked, "But there is no 'eleven' on the phone to dial." Sam just shook his head in disbelief as Geoff looked over at him with raised eyebrows and a knowing smirk on his face. Yup, he heard about that one for weeks after.

By one o'clock Sam wasn't surprised that Trish was late. Grabbing a coffee he decided to sit at the kitchen table and read the newspaper. Sam lived on a two hundred acre ranch that had been in his family for more than a century. It had been handed down from generation to generation and at this moment in family history it was Sam's place. It had a century old log cabin and a barn large enough to hold all the hay and straw that he could harvest each year which he sold to the locals for their cattle or decoration purposes. It wasn't a million dollar business but it paid the bills and kept food in his cupboard.

Foolishly Sam allowed Trish to move into his place six months prior but it wasn't so easy to get her to understand that their relationship wasn't working out and that she had to leave. Once she finally did comprehend, a huge fight ensued with a lot of screaming on her part and a lot of listening on Sam's, until she was done or she just plain exhausted herself, he wasn't sure which. It was during this lull that he suggested she leave right then and there. It hadn't been fun but Sam was glad she was gone and didn't look forward to seeing her again. He had the last of her belongings in boxes just outside the garage door and knew it wouldn't take long to load them up and send her on her way one last time.

Hearing her car pull up Sam threw on his jacket and headed out to the driveway to meet her when he realized it wasn't Trish at all. Sam would recognize that damaged Mustang anywhere. As Sarah got out of her car, he chuckled thinking that, for safety reasons alone, he should keep his distance, just in case.

"Well look who's here! How did you find my place? I suppose A.J. told you." Sam couldn't quite place it but there was something about

Sarah that made him feel like he had known her for a long time. He felt at ease with her. He wasn't sure why but for whatever reason he was definitely happy to see her.

"I must admit you wouldn't have been easy to find but for A.J.'s directions. You live rather remotely don't you? There's nothing around for miles other than a neighbour or two. I'm not so sure I could do it myself. My place is as remote as I would like to get. I can at least walk to my neighbours." Sarah was amazed that Sam's driveway was longer than her whole street.

"True, I am pretty remote but I love it and wouldn't want to live in town. I can breathe out here, my family has lived here for more than a centu…" Sam was cut off by the sound of Trish's car skidding up beside Sarah's, sending a cloud of dust in their direction.

Coughing, Sarah watched with interest as Trish got out of her car. She could tell that this woman, whoever she was, was on a mission. Not even seemingly noticing her, Trish strutted past Sarah and headed directly for Sam.

"Sam! Like, I've been trying to get hold of you for days. Why don't you answer when I call? I mean seriously…." Suddenly noticing Sarah, Trish stopped talking and looked from Sarah to Sam and back again. "Who are you, Honey? I've never seen you before."

Talk about to the point, Sarah thought. *Better still, who the heck are you?* was really what Sarah wanted to say but bit her tongue.

Without waiting for an answer Trish turned to Sam and asked, "Who is she, Sam? Is this your new girlfriend? I can't believe you're already seeing someone else. It's barely been a week since I left."

Ah, now I know who she is. This should be good. Sarah smiled at the thought with renewed interest in this woman.

"Who does that, Sam? I knew you were a complete jerk but seriously couldn't you have at least waited until I had my stuff out of here?" Turning to Sarah she continued, "I don't know who you are, Honey, but I would think twice before getting involved with this jerk."

Raising her eyebrows in surprise by this comment Sarah thought, *First of all, how did I get dragged into this drama? Secondly, go out with him? I don't think so.*

"He has big commitment issues. I mean, seriously, look at me. I'm gorgeous, and this guy kicks me out. Honestly, I don't even know what I saw in him."

"Ah Trish, I'm right here, I can hear you and if I were you, I would load up your boxes and leave while things are still civilized." Sam was already fed up with the way the conversation was going. He just wanted Trish out of his life.

"Go to hell, Sam. Seriously. I was trying to call you to say that I'm keeping Benny and if you think you're getting him you can think again."

Sarah was standing back taking it all in. *This is like a soap opera. Better really. And who the heck is Benny?* Sarah was thoroughly enjoying this. *He seriously hit on her for her looks because she is one good-looking woman. A complete loony but a good looking loony just the same!* But that's where the appeal ended in Sarah's opinion. *I can't wait to see where this is going.*

"Trish!" Sam wanted Trish gone from his life and she just kept hanging on like a leech. "Grab your boxes…no, here, I'll help you load them up because it's time for you to go."

"You don't have to be so rude about it. Seriously. You'll regret this, Sam. You know you'll never find anyone as gorgeous as me again." Looking towards Sarah, Trish added, "No offence, Honey."

CHAPTER ELEVEN

Sarah replied with a smirk, "None taken."

Continuing, Trish looked at Sam and added, "Let's face it, I'm stunning and you know very well that one day you are going to miss all of this," and with that Sarah watched Trish stand sideways in a model type pose with one leg slightly bent, left hand firmly placed on her left hip, right arm pointing straight up in the air and after a few dramatic seconds she dropped both hands to her side, finished with a "Hmmpfh", then turned and walked towards the stack of boxes in front of the garage. Not even looking as she strutted past Sarah, Trish offered, "Good luck with this one, Honey. You're gonna need it."

Sarah just looked at Sam, raised her eyebrows and grinned. She could tell he was regretting this whole encounter but Sarah, was quite frankly, loving the whole thing. *This is hysterical!*

Sam just gave Sarah a blank look, rolled his eyes, sighed and headed over to help Trish load up her boxes.

Watching her finally drive away, all that Sam could think was, *Good riddance!*

From behind him Sarah asked, "So tell me, how the heck does she walk in those four inch stilettos? I'm getting a nose bleed just thinking how high they are."

Sam smiled and turned to look at Sarah with a chuckle, "One time she actually tripped and fell into the duck pond out back. It was sad to see really because once she stood back up she tried to get her shoes unstuck from the muck but the dog came running up trying to lick her face, which was enough on its own to send her over the edge. Trying to push him back made the ducks nearby start quacking and they fluttered away. Well then she really freaked out, screamed and fell flat on her face into the pond again, losing her shoes completely in the muck that time and well...suffice to say that it was not a good night on the ranch. All she could talk about was how she lost her eight hundred dollar designer shoes from New York City in a disgusting duck pond. Who in their right mind pays that kind of money for shoes? Anyway, she carried on and on, saying how it wasn't funny and how I hated her and, well, I could continue but it just isn't worth the energy."

Sarah was laughing out loud at this point. She could picture Trish in her heels walking around a duck pond. *Who does that?* Sarah thought.

She had to admit Trish's make-up was perfect albeit a little heavy on the eye shadow and lipstick and her bright red hair was too poufy and over the top for Sarah but she definitely had a "ten" body. The skinny jeans and low cut top with the cropped jacket looked amazing but those spikes were a little much. She was sharp contrast to Sarah who was wearing sneakers, jeans and a pullover sweater with next to no make-up on. If Trish wore that type of thing out by the duck pond then she deserved to fall in as far as Sarah was concerned. *No woman in her right mind dresses like that on a farm for heaven's sake. I can't imagine how Sam managed to live with someone like her for a day let alone months. Well…judging by her body, I guess I could imagine.*

Sarah looked at Sam and thought that he looked worn out. I'm sure Trish was extremely high maintenance. *If only men like Sam thought from their heart and not their pants, they would end up with someone worth being with….you know…like me.* And quoting Trish, she thought to herself, *After all, they are missing out on all of this!* Smiling, Sarah let her mind retreat back to her time with Travis and how he never really appreciated her and how Gretchen the cheerleader was a blonde bimbo who was likely as high maintenance as Trish. *That's okay, Travis will get what he deserves one day. It's called karma.* Sarah could sense herself getting angry and thought she had better get to the point of why she came here.

"Sam, I stopped by to drop you off a cheque. I was speaking to Mr. Walters, who, by the way, is a very lovely man, and I asked him what he thought it would cost to fix your truck. So I have written a cheque for that amount and if it ends up being more just let me know and I'll get the rest of the money to you right away." Sarah handed Sam the cheque.

"Thanks. Do you want to come in for a coffee? I could use a little relaxation time after Trish. She always was exhausting."

"Um…sure sounds great, thanks Sam!" Following him into the kitchen, Sarah felt a little uncomfortable given their rough start but quickly got past that as soon as she walked into the house. She couldn't help but admire what a nice home he had.

"Your home is amazing, Sam. It has so much character." She was in love with the place already. It had a very large kitchen/living room combination with the ceiling to floor double-sided field stone fireplace being the only partial wall in the centre of the two rooms. The walls and ceiling were log cabin style with a ton of cupboards above and below the kitchen counter and plenty of working counter space. Admiring the stainless steel appliances Sarah couldn't help but be impressed with this kitchen.

The window behind the kitchen sink looked out over the infamous duck pond that Sarah just heard about and there was another window looking to the west of the house with a perfect view of the acreage sprawling out as far as the eye could see. Underneath that window was a comfy looking couch with a coffee table in front of it that looked as if it was at least a hundred years old and hand-cut. There was a big oversized chair directly across from the couch. On the opposite wall was an open concept walk-in pantry. Sarah could barely see some of the jars of preserves lined along the shelves but saw enough to know that it was a good-sized pantry. *I wonder where he gets those preserves. Surely he doesn't do them himself. He must have someone do them for him,* she admired.

To finish things off there was a large, oval, braided, multi-coloured area rug underneath the coffee table that completed the look and gave an overall cozy feel to the room. Sarah wasted no time finding her spot on the couch and settling in with her feet tucked up underneath her.

"This house has been handed down over the generations and no one seemed too anxious to make any big changes to it which I'm really grateful for because I'm happy with it as it is and have no plans for changing anything myself." Sam caught himself looking around the room and admiring some of the little imperfections. The ones that he found comforting as a child were the ones he still found comforting as an adult.

"So, who's Benny? A child?" Sarah inquired.

"Oh God no! Not a kid! Don't get me wrong, I like kids but not with her." He cringed at the thought. "He's a golden retriever dog we adopted together and she may say she's keeping him but he always ends up coming back home to me which drives her crazy but it's nothing that can be controlled. Benny loves it here and no one will stop him from coming back home and she knows it. That's why I didn't worry about arguing that point. She'll find out soon enough."

"Aren't you worried that Benny will get hit by a car finding his way back home?" Sarah was concerned.

"Naw because he never comes here. Trish lives in town not far from the fire hall and Benny always goes straight to the hall, lies down in one of the truck bays and the boys just feed him and give him water until I show up to take him home. Benny's even been known to go right into the firehouse and lie down on the couch and go to sleep. I suppose he's more of a firehouse dog than mine but like I say, she hates dogs anyway. She hates the hair getting on her clothes and she especially hates cleaning up after them. She's just doing this to try and get back at me."

They both laughed when Sarah said, "I can see how Trish and Benny wouldn't exactly be a match made in heaven." Pausing momentarily Sarah added, "It's no fun ending a relationship is it, Sam? I've been there done that but you seem to be able to control your temper which I have a harder time doing as I'm sure you noticed." Smiling sheepishly Sarah continued, "Don't you think she was a little young for you anyway, Sam? I mean she looks like she's about twenty-five and you're what? Late thirties?"

Handing Sarah her coffee Sam smiled, "You're close, I'm thirty-six but in fact you are wrong, Trish is thirty-five years old trying to be a twenty-five year old and I guess succeeding by what you tell me. No, she's not too young, just too attractive for my own good, although it didn't take long for that attraction to lose its lustre." Sam wasn't sure why he felt so comfortable speaking to Sarah about his personal life but the words just seemed to flow. "So Sarah, what's your story? What brought you to Forestville?" Sam was curious.

"Just needed a change of scenery really." Sarah didn't want to get into the whole discussion of Travis. She just wanted to put that relationship behind her and talking about it was only going to dredge up the hurt.

"Well, I don't believe that. What was his name?" Sam speculated a guy was involved and judging by her response, it didn't go well.

Sarah quickly looked up at Sam. "What makes you ask *that*?" She felt a bit uncomfortable talking about Travis with Sam. Truth be told, she felt a bit uncomfortable talking about Travis at all.

"Come on, you're not fooling me but hey no worries if you don't want to talk about it. That's your business." Sam could tell she was hiding something but let it drop and took a sip of coffee.

Sarah gave Sam a good-humoured look of annoyance and then laughed it off. She couldn't explain it but it just felt right sitting here in Sam's kitchen, talking over coffee. Like she belonged.

After a few minutes she decided to elaborate.

"It's funny, he's the first guy I ever became serious with. I thought I was madly in love. He could do no wrong in my eyes and I foolishly put all my trust in him. It was great at first but in time he let his football career cloud his judgement and his ego took precedence over me." Sarah was staring out the window at this point reflecting back.

Sam could see the hurt in her eyes but said nothing.

"Anyway you don't need to hear my sob story."

"Hey listen, I'm here, you're talking. Carry on."

Feeling a little embarrassed Sarah hesitated to continue but something compelled her to.

"Well, long story short, Travis, that's his name, ended up cheating on me with a cheerleader and I left. So there you go, pathetic right? Same sad story everyone has and so I'm here trying to get back on my feet." She spoke without thinking. "I'm not the easiest person to handle sometimes." Then realizing what she said Sarah quickly looked over at Sam.

"Really? I would never have guessed," he chuckled.

Giving him a playful snide look, Sarah continued. "My father thinks I'm not tough enough at times on someone like Travis and my mother claims I'm a little too outspoken and short-tempered." Rolling her eyes she sighed. "Either way the bastard cheated on me, I left and I hope I never hear from him again." That comment rang truer than Sarah cared to admit.

Sitting quietly for a few minutes and absorbing what Sarah just told him, Sam added, "Ah well, sounds like Travis is an asshole." And with that they both laughed.

"That he is." Sarah confirmed.

After finishing his coffee Sam said, "Well I must get going into town. Trish was supposed to be here by noon and leave it to her to keep me waiting. Old Bill and I are going to play poker with the boys and it's at a buddy's place tonight. I told Bill I would pick him up so we could head over for an early steak dinner at the Old Beagle beforehand."

Walking Sarah out to her car Sam thanked her for coming by. "You managed to come at the perfect time, it kept things civilized when Trish showed up. Thanks for that."

"Anytime Sam. She was an interesting person to meet and I think in the end you will both be better off apart. Just promise me one thing. The next time you ask a girl out, make sure it's for her personality. I know that's unheard of in the 'guy code' but believe it or not you end up with someone you will actually be able to carry an intellectual conversation with," and laughing Sarah got into her car and headed down Sam's rather long driveway and for home.

Well Sarah, I just may have to take your advice, Sam thought with a smile as he watched her drive away. Glancing down at the ground Sam saw one of Trish's shoes, the big tall expensive spikey ones she loved so much. It had fallen out of one of the boxes. Picking it up he thought, *I know exactly what to do with this*, and laughing, walked around the house and tossed it into the pond. *Adios Trish!*

TWELVE

That night, Sarah could tell summer had ended by the obvious chill in the air. The leaves changing colour confirmed it. George started a fire outside in the fire pit near the water and set up chairs for the two ladies and him. Sarah told her mother to head outside while she made coffee.

"I'll be out shortly, Mom. You go and relax outside with Dad."

Sarah was looking forward to a nice relaxing evening with her parents. However, while making coffee the telephone rang and Sarah regretted answering immediately upon saying hello. It was Travis again.

"Hey Baby, how's it goin'? Been writing on any cars lately? When are you coming home so I can thank you in person for the note you left me?"

"Travis, why are you calling me again? You know I'm never coming back." Sarah was annoyed but spoke quietly so her parents wouldn't overhear.

"You're a real piece of work you know that, Sarah? I said I was sorry but that isn't good enough for you is it? What's your problem? People make mistakes."

"Travis, I'm not your baby and you got what you deserved and if you know what's good for you then you won't call me again." She was starting to raise her voice.

"Well Baby, if you won't come to me…well then, I guess I'm gonna have to come to you. You cost me big bucks and you're gonna pay…"

Hanging up on Travis, Sarah was shaken by the phone call. She thought she knew Travis well enough to know that he would never threaten to hurt her but she was feeling more uncomfortable with each conversation they had.

"Sarah? Where are you, dear?" Karen called.

"Coming Mom! Just getting the coffee." She tried not to sound upset. She didn't want her parents worrying about her. She could handle Travis. Well, at least she was pretty sure she could. *Sarah, you know Travis better than that. He would never do anything to hurt you. He's just trying to scare you. C'mon girl get it together.* Shaking off any concern she had, Sarah grabbed her jacket and headed outside where her parents had already settled in to enjoy the evening. Offering them both a coffee she sat down and enjoyed the warmth emanating from the fire. In the distance a loon echoed and she could hear the water lapping against the shore. Drawing a deep breath Sarah relaxed and knew that this was exactly where she needed to be.

"Sarah dear, where did you go today? When we returned after lunch from Terri's you were gone." Karen was curious to know.

"Oh I went out of town to a friend of A.J.'s. You know, the guy whose truck I hit. After I picked up the groceries the other morning, I went to the garage to see what it was going to cost to have it fixed and decided to take him a cheque today so he would have it when he picked up his truck." Sarah took another sip of her coffee and smiled.

"You should have been there, it was hysterical. His ex-girlfriend showed up and what a piece of work she was!" Sarah went on to explain what happened with Trish and had her parents laughing until they cried. "It was so funny to hear her say how stunning she was! Honestly, I thought I was going to burst out laughing right then and there!"

"I thought that you didn't like this Sam character. Didn't you say he was, how did you put it, a raving lunatic?" her father asked.

"Oh for sure when I first met him, but once we got to know each other at Terri's, I realized he really wasn't a bad guy after all. A bit stupid in the women department but not a bad guy."

"So, why don't you go out with him, dear?" her mother asked.

"Mother! What the heck are you talking about? First of all, I just broke up with Travis which was a complete nightmare and secondly, if he was at all interested, which I'm sure he's not, he knows where to find me."

Sarah was shocked her mother would even suggest such a ridiculous thing. *I mean Sam is nice and all but I'm not interested. Well, I suppose I could be interested. He is quite handsome. But I'm not ready for another man in my life quite yet. At least I don't think I am. But if I were, then Sam would definitely be a good option...well, the only option at this point really. It's a ridiculous thought anyway. Mom honestly doesn't know when to let up. She's determined to get me married off as quickly as possible. Well that's just a crazy thought, going out with Sam. He may not even be interested anyway. Although I don't see why he wouldn't be, after all he's missing out on all of this!* Chuckling to herself, Sarah's thoughts were interrupted by her mother.

"Sarah! You're not listening to me, dear. Where the heck is your head at?" her mother sounded frustrated.

"Oh sorry, Mom. I was just thinking about a few things. What did you say?" Sarah tried to stay focussed.

"I asked you why you aren't interested in this fellow? I'm sure he's a lovely person if he's A.J.'s best friend. I mean after all, dear, you aren't as young as you used to be...."

"Karen, for chrissakes leave the girl alone." George hated when Karen tried to play matchmaker. She was always butting into the girls' lives and it drove him crazy and he was sure the girls weren't so fond of it either.

"Now George, it is my business. I want to be sure both of our girls are taken care of by nice young men. It's such a worry to have Sarah living by herself. And besides, she isn't getting any younger..." Karen tried to impress her opinion on George.

"Mom. I'm right here." Sarah was mortified at her mother's comments.

"Karen, quit matchmaking and let's just enjoy the nice night and fire. I know I don't want to discuss Sarah's love life right now and I'm getting the impression she doesn't either."

George must have made his point because Karen stopped talking and stared into the fire with a heavy sigh. Sarah looked at her father and mouthed the words 'Thank you' to him when her mother wasn't looking. He just smiled and poked the fire with a stick. The remainder of the evening was peaceful and relaxing. The conversation took on a lighter air and discussion revolved around why Grandma got mad at Grandpa for planting cherry tomato plants and not beefsteak; how Aunt Patty went to get her hair coloured at a discount salon and came out crying because they coloured it bright orange and how cousin Max was pulled over by the police for speeding and started giving the cop a hard time and was thrown in jail overnight.

Sarah was thoroughly enjoying hearing all about the family drama. She missed home and most especially her mom and dad. It was heaven sitting around the fire with them sharing a few laughs. They had only been there for a couple of days but Sarah found herself already wishing that they didn't have to leave in a couple of weeks. *I really must speak to them about staying*, she thought to herself.

THIRTEEN

Come Sunday morning A.J., Old Bill, 'the kid', Geoff and Rudy sat at the Old Beagle having coffee awaiting Sam's arrival.

"Good morning, Boys! So what's good on the menu today?" Sam asked as he walked in and sat down at the table.

"Hey thar, Sam, how're yer doin'?", Old Bill asked and nudged the kid who begrudgingly conceded with a snarky, "Hi."

"Hey Sam," the rest of the gang pitched in.

Sam was surprised to see Will and then remembered that his dad, Marty, had told him that during his six month time with Bill he had to participate in everything Bill did including community service. Sam chuckled. The kid looked completely bored and miserable sitting with a bunch of old guys at such an early hour on a Sunday morning. *I'm sure all he wanted to do was sleep in till noon. Aw well, the kid is getting what he deserves.*

Old Bill signalled for the waitress to come to the table. "I don't know what yer boys are havin' but I'm havin' the Old Beagle Special. Gotta love those three eggs, bacon, sausage, hash browns, toast and coffee and by God I'm gittin' hungry just thinkin' about it."

After placing their orders, the waitress topped them up with coffee and A.J. got down to business.

"Okay, first of all, I want to say thanks to Rudy for volunteering to help us out with the parade this year."

"No problem A.J.," Rudy responded.

"As most of you know, I met with Town Council last week regarding the Santa Claus parade and there are a few changes this year. Firstly, it has been decided that the Santa Claus parade will now be called the Christmas Eve parade and will be held…well, on Christmas Eve starting at 7 o'clock that night."

"What? Since when do we hold the parade on Christmas Eve?", Geoff asked. "Most people have church to attend, family get-togethers and dinners. I think that's a mistake."

"Well, I don't disagree with you, Geoff, but that's Council's decision so we, as the organizers, need to make this work." A.J. continued. "We have a lot of work ahead of us to get this organized and we need to figure out who will be in charge of what so we can get started right away. I know it's only September but the time will go by quickly. Now, I have a list of jobs and you can let me know who wants to do what. Will, I'm going to need you to recruit some of the high school kids to help with crowd control. You all need your community hours anyway, so this is as good a time as any to get them."

Old Bill gently kicked the kid under the table to get his attention away from his fascination with the top of the table they were sitting at. The kid jumped to attention and mundanely responded, "Yeah okay."

In no time at all A.J. had all the jobs distributed and with breakfast almost done they discussed the finer details.

"Well, that hit the spot.", Sam said wiping his mouth with a napkin. Dropping it onto his plate he asked, "Now if I'm going to be in charge of recruiting and organizing floats and getting the firefighters to participate with the trucks, then I need to have some help. Who here is going to give me a hand?" Looking around the table no one seemed too eager to take on the challenge.

"Not me, Sammy boy.", Geoff piped up right away. "I have enough to organize with the parade fundraising, I don't need anything else to do. What about you, Bill? Why don't you and the kid here help Sam?"

"Sorry Sam, I have the shop ta run and now I need ta organize the service groups around town ta supply food and hot chocolate at the community centre after the parade. Plus I have ta arrange fer volunteers ta help with that. Nope, count me out and the kid too."

Bill leaned back and took another drink of his coffee and purposely nudged the kid's arm at the same time, which brought the kid to attention once again with a, "Yeah whatever." Bill chuckled at the sad sight beside him.

"Geez boys, don't all jump in at once to offer some help here. What about you, Rudy? You don't seem to be doing all that much, you can help me." Sam leaned forward looking at Rudy who managed to quickly choke down what pancakes he had in his mouth.

"Sure Sam, I could help you except I need to worry about getting the flyers out to all of the businesses in town. Plus I'm helping A.J. recruit for crowd control now and I have to help build a float for the public school where Deb teaches. She practically threatened me within an inch of my life if I didn't help them put a float together. Well, she didn't threaten my physical life…it was my sex life and quite frankly Sam, that's more important to me than helping you. So nope, I'm out buddy!" and with that Rudy continued to eat his pancakes which seemed to take the guy forever Sam thought. *I've never seen anyone eat so goddamned much and so goddamned slow in all my life.* Leaning back in his chair Sam was getting irritated.

"The hell with all you assholes!"

They all started laughing, with Sam joining in. He knew before he even asked that he wouldn't get any help from them but as far as he was concerned it didn't hurt to try.

FOURTEEN

THE FIRST WEEK OF SARAH's parents visiting had gone by quickly. It had been filled with unpacking boxes, moving furniture around, setting up the kitchen cupboards and meals with Terri and A.J. Sarah couldn't believe her parents would have to leave in another week. She would be sad to see them go. It was nice having them around.

It was Saturday afternoon. The day had gone by so fast that Sarah couldn't believe it was almost time for dinner. She decided to finish unpacking the box of clothes she had just opened up and then get dinner started. Traditionally in their family, Saturday nights were homemade pizza nights and Sarah could hardly wait for tonight's dinner. From the bedroom, she smiled listening to her parents talking down the hall.

"Karen, where in hell is my toolbox?", George hollered from the living room.

"It's in the basement, George."

"Karen! For God sake where is my toolbox? It was right here and now it's gone. So where is it?" George was getting more frustrated by the second. "Karen!!"

"George, I said it was in the basement, dear. Why all the yelling?" Karen headed towards the living room to see her husband. Storming out of the living room, George walked right into Karen nearly knocking her over.

"What the...? Weren't you just in the kitchen a minute ago? You could give a guy a heart attack. Are you trying to kill me?" George started to rant and Karen just shook her head and laughed.

"Why are you laughing? Is it funny to think I could be dead right now, Karen? Is it funny to think that you could have been responsible for becoming a widow? Well, get your laughs in now, Karen, get them in now because you won't be laughing at my funeral." And with that George headed to the garage to look for his toolbox.

"George?"

"What!" Stopping at the side door he looked back at Karen who pointed to the basement door.

"Your toolbox is in the basement." Chuckling, Karen always knew when George was getting frustrated with something he was working on and his ranting was just his way of letting off steam and never something she took offence to. Heading down the hallway Karen found Sarah in her bedroom sorting through clothing.

"Hey Mom, what's wrong with Dad?" Sarah was picking up each article of clothing and holding it up for inspection.

"Oh, nothing, dear, you know how he gets when he's frustrated. He's trying to get the TV mounted on the wall, set up the Bluray player and the surround sound but the bookcase is in his way. I don't think things are working out how he hoped. He'll figure it out though. You know your dad, there's always hell to pay when things aren't going well."

CHAPTER FOURTEEN

"Do you think he needs help moving the bookcase?" Sarah was concerned because it was a solid oak bookcase and knew it was likely too heavy for one person to be moving around.

"No I don't think so, Sarah. Best to let him work it out on his own and if he needs help he'll say so. Save us both from getting yelled at." Both women laughed out loud and continued putting away clothes.

Several minutes later, they were startled by a large crash from the living room. Both women ran down the hall to see what was going on. Seeing what happened, Sarah ran to the phone and Karen ran over to help George.

"Oh my God, George! Sarah! Call an ambulance, your father's unconscious!" Karen immediately started crying. Sarah quickly called 9-1-1.

"Yes operator, please send an ambulance to 13692 Lakeshore Road. A bookcase fell over onto my father and it looks like he's also hit his head on the coffee table when he fell. His head is bleeding and he's unconscious! Please hurry!" Even though she was frantic on the inside, Sarah somehow managed to remain calm on the outside.

Hanging up, she ran back into the living room and with the help of her mother somehow managed to slide the bookcase off her father. *Dammit, I should never have let Dad do this alone. It was way too big for one person to manage.* Although it was a gift from her parents, Sarah was regretting having it, but when she saw how distraught her mother was she stopped reprimanding herself. Putting her arm around her mother's shoulders, Sarah tried to calmly reason with her.

"Mom, go get a blanket to cover Dad and bring me a towel for his head as well." Karen just sat on the floor beside George crying inconsolably.

"Mom! I'm telling you right now, stop crying and go get a blanket and a towel. You can't help him by sitting there crying. He'll be fine. I called for an ambulance and they'll be here shortly." Kneeling on the floor in front of her mother Sarah placed her hands on her mother's shoulders to draw her attention away from her father. Looking at Sarah, Karen had tears streaming down her face. Sarah felt sick seeing her mother this way.

"Mom. Dad will be okay. Please just go get a blanket so we can keep him warm and a towel so that I can help stop the bleeding until the ambulance comes." Something in Sarah's commanding voice caught Karen's attention and she nodded her head in reply while Sarah helped her to her feet.

In the distance Sarah could hear the sirens and was relieved to know they were on their way. Returning with the blanket and towel Karen handed them to Sarah who suggested her mother sit down on the couch while she took care of her father. Covering him with a blanket Sarah sat on the floor beside her father and held the towel firmly to his head to try and control the bleeding. George moaned in pain and started to rock his head back and forth.

"Dad? Oh my God! Dad?" Inside Sarah was numb but she knew she had to remain calm for her father's sake and more importantly for her mother's sake right now. Her mother never coped well during an emergency however Sarah thankfully inherited her sense of calm from her father. The sirens were getting closer. Sarah looked at her mother who was sitting on the couch crying.

"Mom you need to stay calm right now okay? Where's Dad's health card? The paramedics are going to need it for the hospital."

Not answering immediately, Karen finally found her voice. "It's in your father's wallet on the dresser in the guest room."

"Mom, I need you to go get it right now for me okay? Right now, Mom."

Nodding, Karen got George's health card and returned to the living room. After the ambulance pulled into her driveway Sarah heard the paramedics call out as they came into the house. She shouted for them to come into the living room. As they appeared, she was relieved to see a familiar face and tears immediately came to her eyes.

FIFTEEN

"SAM, WHY ARE YOU HERE? Why is the Fire Department here?" Sarah was a little confused.

"There are no ambulance stations close by and so the firefighters have been trained to deal with medical calls until an ambulance arrives." Getting to the point quickly Sam asked, "What's going on?"

It took all Sarah had to control her emotions to answer. "It's my dad. He's been hurt."

At first glance Sam knew her father was not in good shape. He had no colour in his face; his breathing was shallow and laboured with minimal movement and judging by the blood, he had hit his head. On the couch, Sam could see another woman sobbing uncontrollably and assumed it was Sarah's mother.

"Here, Sarah, we can take care of your Dad now. Why don't you go wash your hands while we assess him." Sam offered, taking the towel from her. As the other firefighters assessed George, Sam waited for Sarah to return and then took down the details and circumstances surrounding what happened. As Sarah filled Sam in he could tell she was barely keeping it together. But she was, and her strength impressed him.

"Ward, did you get the details? I hear Davis pulling into the driveway with the ambulance. I'm confident the patient is stable enough to be transported immediately." Maury confirmed. Maury Spencer had been a full-time firefighter for fifteen years and a Captain for ten and Sam trusted him. He was like an icon to the guys at the hall. If Maury said it was so, it was gospel.

"Yeah Captain, done." Sam closed his notebook and headed to the side door to greet Larry Davis and his partner Matt. Calling out the door Sam shouted, "In here guys!"

"Hey Sam, how's it goin'? Where to?" Larry was pushing a gurney with the defibrillator and medical bag with Matt following close behind.

"In the living room to the right there." Sam pointed him in the direction where Maury and Geoff were still tending to George.

"What have we got here, Captain?"

Maury explained the situation to Larry and then deferred to Sam who filled him in on the details he had documented. After Larry assessed George, he was placed onto the gurney and prepared for transport to the hospital.

"Hey Larry, can someone ride with him?" Sam asked because he was pretty sure Sarah or her mother would want to.

"Yup, but they have to come now. We don't have time to wait, Sam." Larry pushed the gurney out to the ambulance while Sam held back to speak with Sarah.

"Sarah, your mom can ride with your dad in the back but I'm thinking maybe you should because your mom seems pretty upset." Sam looked at Karen who was standing just outside the back door watching as they wheeled George out to the ambulance.

CHAPTER FIFTEEN

Sarah looked at her mother and contemplated what to do. Walking over to speak with her Sarah asked, "Mom, they've said that you can ride with dad in the ambulance. Would you like to do that?" Sarah stood in front of her mother to get her full attention. Holding her hands in her own, she looked sympathetically into her mother's eyes. She had never seen her mom so upset before and wasn't quite sure how to deal with it. Inside Sarah was ready to fall apart. It frightened her to see her dad hurt and unable to help himself. *Dad's always the strong one. He's always the one who helps everyone else but he looked so weak and frail.* Sarah shook herself from her own thoughts when her mother nodded her head yes.

"Yes dear, I would like to go with your father," and with that Karen started to cry again.

"But, here's the thing, Mom. If you want to ride with Dad you have to stop crying and get some control because you will only upset him and that's not what we want right now. Dad needs you to stay strong and you need to stop crying. Do you understand me?" Sarah pleaded with her mom.

Karen started to settle down, listening to her daughter. Blinking the tears from her eyes she stopped crying, nodded and said, "Yes, I understand. I'll do that, I promise."

"Sam! Let's go! Do we have a rider or not?" Maury was shouting from the driveway. Sam looked at Sarah who nodded her head. "Coming Captain!" Sam put his arm around Karen and quietly said, "Okay let's go so you can keep your husband company."

Leading her gently out and into the ambulance, Sam shut the door with a bang, pounded the back of the ambulance twice to let Davis know he could move and with that the siren started and they left. Turning to head back to the house, Captain Spencer signalled for Sam to hop in the truck so they could head out. "Just give me a sec, Captain."

Sam called and headed to the house where he saw Sarah standing in the kitchen looking lost and a little pathetic at this particular moment.

"Sarah? You okay?" Sam walked over to check on her and noticed she was shaking. *Oh boy. This girl may go into shock. Shit!*

"Captain, we need to stay a few more minutes." Sam shouted. Going into the living room he found the blanket, went back and wrapped it around Sarah who took it willingly. Leading her to a kitchen chair he gently guided her down to sit. She wasn't crying but she was definitely not very responsive right now.

"Do you think he'll make it, Sam?" Sarah asked calmly, almost without emotion.

"He seems like a tough guy." Sam felt sorry for her. She was a tough girl herself but she looked pretty vulnerable right now. Grabbing a glass of water and a chair, Sam handed Sarah the drink as he sat down in front of her.

"Sarah, how are you getting to the hospital? You can't drive yourself, do you want me to call A.J. and Terri to come and get you?"

"Um, sure Sam, that would be great." Sarah took a sip of water. "Oh wait. I forgot. Terri and A.J. are at a fundraiser tonight in Mobridge. Is that anywhere near the hospital?"

"They've taken your dad to Dockside which is about 15 minutes away from here but in the opposite direction. I'll give A.J. a call on his cell and let them know to go straight to the hospital. In the meantime, I'm going to speak to the Captain to see if I can drive you because you are in no shape to be driving yourself. I'll be right back." And with that Sam went outside and returned in what seemed to Sarah like seconds.

"All clear, since I'm only here as a volunteer tonight. The guys said to leave my bunker gear with them so I can take you straight from here.

Where's your coat?" Sarah told Sam where her coat and purse were and grabbing a coat for her mother Sam got into the driver's side of Sarah's car. Backing out of the driveway Sam teased, "So this is the beast that hit my brand new truck. We need to talk." Sam was relieved to see Sarah smile.

Arriving at the emergency department, Sarah looked around for her mother but couldn't see her. Sam spoke to the triage nurse after which he indicated for Sarah to follow him. Finding her mother, Sarah was updated that her father was conscious. He was getting x-rays and would be back soon.

It wasn't long before A.J. and Terri arrived. Terri had obviously been crying on the way and was frantic by the time they arrived.

"Mom, Sarah, how's Dad? Where is he? Is he going to make it?"

A.J. walked up to Sam and shook his hand thanking him for the call and for bringing Sarah to the hospital.

Within the hour the doctor came to advise that George required several stitches in his head. He also confirmed that x-rays indicated George had sustained three broken ribs and a fractured rib but thankfully no punctured lung.

"He's also suffered a mild concussion. He's lucky. It could have been a lot worse. Why don't you all go grab a coffee and someone will be around to get you once George is ready to go." Once updated, everyone seemed to relax and headed to the hospital coffee shop.

Sipping on a coffee, Karen was finally snapping out of her emotional distress and realized that she hadn't been introduced to Sam.

"Sarah, who's your friend?" Karen seemed especially interested because he was a handsome young man and looked rather promising as a potential suitor for Sarah.

"Mother, Sam's not my friend." Sarah retorted, a little too quickly.

"Well, thanks." Sam feigned hurt feelings and everyone laughed except Sarah who started to blush.

"Well, he is my friend…sort of. That is to say, I just met him. He's my friend but he's actually A.J. and Terri's friend and we weren't friends but I suppose we are friends…now." Sarah couldn't believe how tongue-tied she had become and it was uncomfortable. A.J. and Terri laughed as all eyes turned to Sam who was grinning with amusement. Then, finding this all rather entertaining, they turned back to Sarah as she struggled with words, buckling to the pressure she was suddenly feeling.

"So, I'm confused, Sarah. Are we friends, or aren't we?" Sam purposely added to Sarah's discomfort.

"Ohhh, so you're Sarah's Sam!" Karen was especially interested in this young man now.

"Mother, don't say it like that! You're embarrassing me." Sarah was mortified. Sam was the last person Sarah wanted her mother to try and set her up with. *Honestly, we're just friends and barely friends at that. Sam and I would mix like oil and water, although, I must admit he has grown on me recently, and he really is a good looking guy and he does have stunning blue eyes. How come I've never noticed his eyes before? Wow, the blue is even more emphasized with that shirt he's wearing...hmmm...funny I've never noticed…*

Sarah suddenly realized that she had been staring at Sam and even worse, that he noticed and was looking back at her, eyebrows raised with a smirk on his face. Winking knowingly at Sarah, Sam turned to Karen.

CHAPTER FIFTEEN

"Why, what has she told you about me?" Sam was purposely fishing because he knew Sarah wouldn't want it and he was having a little fun at her expense. A.J. and Terri were laughing and thoroughly enjoying the scene unfolding before them. As far as they were concerned it looked good on Sarah.

Sarah sunk down in her chair and could feel herself turning shades of red from the embarrassment she felt. *My mother really must learn to shut the hell up,* she thought. Just then her phone rang and Sarah gladly grabbed the opportunity to walk away hoping the conversation would revert away from her while she was gone. Sitting at a table where she wouldn't be overheard, Sarah answered the phone, "Hello, Sarah here."

"How's your dad doing, Sarah?"

Sarah hung up immediately. *This is getting scary now. How does he know about Dad? He couldn't possibly know unless…* Looking around for any sign of Travis, Sarah felt uncomfortable. As much as she was trying to fight it she was finding herself frightened by Travis' unnerving phone calls. He was almost obsessed.

"Sarah! Let's go, we can take Dad home now." Terri called out across the cafeteria.

"Okay Terri! You guys go ahead and I'll meet up with you at the car. I just need to make a phone call first." Waiting until she saw that everyone had left, Sarah dialled Travis' mobile.

"I see you changed your mind, baby." Travis' arrogant voice echoed across the line.

"Now listen, Travis. I'm only going to say this once, and you had better hear me loud and clear. I am *not* coming back to you; I do *not* have a new boyfriend; I said I would pay for the damages and I am telling you one last time – stop phoning me! Your idle threats are just becoming annoying, as are you. I've had enough of you trying to intimidate me! I'm not sure why or how you are spying on me but I'm not afraid of you, Travis!" Sarah was shaking like a leaf as she spoke. "If you keep calling me I'll get the police involved. Are we perfectly clear?" Silence. "Travis?"

"That was a lovely speech, Sarah. I'll be in touch again soon, baby," and with that Travis hung up the phone.

Collapsing into a chair, it had taken all her remaining energy to keep Travis from realizing just how frightened she actually was. *Maybe that will be the last I hear from him,* she tried to convince herself, although something told her this was only wishful thinking. Doing her best to fight back tears that were threatening to come, Sarah took a moment to gather her wits about her and then headed to the car.

SIXTEEN

It took a couple of days before Sarah's dad was even able to get out of bed. The doctor warned that he would still have to be careful, with absolutely no heavy lifting or any light lifting for that matter.

"I'm sorry, Sarah, dear. Your father really should be at home and go see his own doctor. We promise to come back in a few weeks when he's feeling better."

Karen gave her daughter a big hug and said that she was going to go and pack up their things. After some urging for them to stay Sarah conceded that it was likely best for her parents to go home where her dad could recover in the comfort of his own bed. Sarah couldn't help but be disappointed about them leaving, firstly because her dad was hurt and secondly because they had just arrived.

Still in a great deal of pain George sat down at the kitchen table.

"Now tell me, Kiddo. Has that no good football player been in contact with you about his car yet?", George winced as he tried to adjust his position.

"No Daddy…why do you keep asking me that?" Sarah tried not to sound defensive. She hated lying to her dad about Travis but didn't want to worry him especially when he wasn't well.

"Well, if he does, Sarah, don't you deal with him. You be sure to tell A.J. and let him deal with that sorry son-of-a-bitch. Understand?" George winced again.

"Yes, Daddy, I understand."

"Also, I'm leaving all my tools here because your mother and I will be back in a few weeks, after Thanksgiving, and I'm going to finish up what I started before that damned bookcase fell on me."

"George, where's your wallet?" Karen called out from the bedroom. Sarah laughed to herself because her father was famous for putting his wallet everywhere and it was always a mystery where he would put it next.

"For God's sake, Karen, you were the last one with it. I'm sure you said you put it in my coat pocket for safe keeping." George was obviously in a lot of pain. Turning to Sarah, he continued.

"Now, I started to do some rewiring in the basement and have some of the wires hanging down from the ceiling which need to be capped off with the orange wire connectors I have down there. You can do that. The caps are on the big window ledge. Everything else can wait until I get back."

George tried to stand up but the pain was excruciating. Sarah could tell by the look on his face that he was in more pain than he was admitting. She quickly jumped up to assist him putting her left arm around his waist and helped him to his feet. "Damn this is frustrating!" George blurted out.

"Okay dear, I have everything packed. Sarah, would you mind helping your father to the car. I can grab our suitcases." Sarah could tell her mother was concerned about her dad – the worry on her face said it all.

CHAPTER SIXTEEN

Having helped her dad into the front seat, Sarah turned to her mother and gave her a hug.

"Bye, Mom. Make sure you let me know what Daddy's doctor has to say after his check-up."

"Don't worry, dear, I'll be sure to let you know. He'll be fine. He just needs time to heal. I love you, Sarah."

"I love you too, Mom." And with a quick honk of the horn they were gone. Sarah was sad to see them leave but grateful they would be back in a few weeks.

Watching her parents drive away, Sarah felt lonely and wasn't quite sure what to do with herself. *Funny how quickly one can adapt to having company around the house.* Sighing, she decided to keep herself busy unpacking more of the seemingly endless supply of moving boxes.

SEVENTEEN

The next day, Sarah decided to enjoy the morning sun out on the dock with a cup of coffee. The last week had been stressful and some quiet time by the water would be just the thing she needed to relax.

Walking back to the house, Sarah was surprised to see Sam pull into her driveway. Waving, he got out of the car and headed her way.

"Hi Sam! Come on in…would you like a coffee?" Wrapping her sweater tighter around her, Sarah shivered against the cool morning breeze. "I can't believe how fast it seems to be cooling down now." Pausing, Sarah added, "Sam, I want to say thanks again for all your help with my dad the other day. It meant a lot to my family and me."

"Anytime, Sarah. I'm just glad he's going to be okay. Where is he now?"

"They went home yesterday. Mom wants him to see his own doctor and sleep in his own bed. She feels he will recuperate better at home which she's probably right about." Sarah poured Sam a coffee and passed it to him.

"So what brings you here this morning?" Sarah was curious to know.

"Well, I came to ask a favour. I figure you owe me after wrecking my new truck..." Grinning Sam wasn't serious but figured it couldn't hurt his cause. He really needed help with the parade and although his intention wasn't originally to recruit Sarah, he figured he had nothing to lose by asking.

Sarah couldn't help but melt a little at the sight of his sheepish grin. *He really is quite charming and quite good-looking.*

"Well, I can't argue with you over that. I suppose I am indebted to you in some small way after your truck and now my dad. So what's the favour?" She knew Sam was kidding around but was eager to help him with whatever he needed.

"I'm on the committee for the Christmas parade this year and I need a hand with recruiting and organizing all the floats prior to the day. I was wondering if you would be interested in helping me out this year?"

"Sure, why not? Sounds like fun!" Grabbing another coffee, Sarah sat down at the table. "What do you need me to do?" Sarah listened intently as Sam explained what needed to get done.

"And we have just over two months to do it." Sam finished up.

"Well I suppose I had better have something to keep me busy and out of trouble or A.J. will lock me away."

Laughing they spent the next several hours discussing the Christmas parade and how to tackle the issue of Joe at Joe's Hardware. Apparently, Joe didn't like to hand over his money on the best of days and especially hated anything to do with Christmas. As a result he always refused to participate in the parade. Sarah happily offered to tackle Joe this year.

Checking the time, Sam finished up his coffee and got up to leave.

"Well I had better get going. Thanks again, Sarah. I'll be in touch with you after my day shift next week."

CHAPTER SEVENTEEN

Waving good-bye, Sarah was disappointed to see him leave. She had enjoyed his company and although she almost hated to admit it, she quite liked Sam.

EIGHTEEN

WITH THE DAY SHIFT JUST about over, Sam had to concede that as happy as he was to be full-time at the fire hall now, the week at work had been a tough one. Spud had been more of an asshole than usual this shift and as if on cue, the 'thorn in Sam's side' still wasn't finished with him.

"Ward! What in hell are you doing? I said to get the hose lines off that truck and start folding them!" Spud was in fine form again today and Sam had been trying unsuccessfully to stay off his hit list.

Shoving the last of the hose back onto the truck, Sam finally headed to his locker, changed and went to the Old Beagle to meet up with the crew. Thursday nights were pub nights for the firefighters and after this shift Sam needed a beer or two.

"What's up, Boys?" Sam asked as he joined the group and flagged the waitress down to order a beer.

"There he is. How's it going with Spud?" Geoff laughed knowing full well it had been a tough shift for Sam with the Captain.

"Shut the hell up, Geoff." Sam feigned anger but joined the rest of his friends laughing over his misfortunes at work. "It was just my luck to end up on the crew with Spud as my Captain. I would have preferred to be on Maury Spencer's crew."

"What the hell did you do to piss Spud off this time?" Rudy asked.

"I have no idea, Rudy." Sam relented.

"Hey Sam. Isn't that your girlfriend coming in the door?" John asked.

Looking, Sam saw Sarah standing just inside the door gazing around as if looking for someone in particular. Catching sight of Sam she smiled and waved.

"Invite her over, Sam. We'd like to meet the woman who dared smash into your brand new truck." John egged Sam on.

Calling Sarah over, Sam introduced her to the group.

"Don't believe a damn word they say about me, Sarah. They'll say anything to charm a beautiful woman…I mean…they'll say anything to charm you." Sam stumbled over his words but Sarah had been oblivious to what was said. "What brings you here?" he was curious.

"Supposedly A.J. and Terri but they aren't here yet." Sarah gave the room a quick scan but saw no sign of her sister and brother-in-law.

Standing up, Geoff offered his hand to Sarah. "Hi Sarah, I'm Geoff! Why don't you sit here beside me, there's lots of room."

"Rookie. Give the lady your chair." Grabbing the back of John's chair, Geoff tipped it, sending John onto the floor and placed it back down beside him for Sarah.

"What the hell!" John was less than pleased but stood up and grabbed another chair from a nearby table and sat down again.

CHAPTER EIGHTEEN

"What would you like to drink? It's on me." Geoff was very interested in Sarah.

Sarah appeared to be the hit of the party with the firefighters. Sam could barely get a word in edgewise. And as far as Sam was concerned, Geoff was a little too interested in Sarah but what was even more irritating was that Sarah seemed to be enjoying the attention.

"You know, Sarah, I'd be happy to show you around the area if you are free on Saturday. I'm not working and afterwards we could grab a bite to eat at the Mountain Lake restaurant, just a few miles out of town."

"What the hell, Geoff!" All eyes turned to Sam with everyone waiting for him to continue.

Rudy sat back and laughed as he listened to the commentary between Sam and Geoff. *This is getting interesting,* he thought, taking another drink of his beer.

Realizing his mistake Sam cleared his throat and tried to backtrack. "I mean…um…Sarah can't go Saturday…" Sam searched for the right words.

"Really Sam? How would you know? I think Sarah can speak for herself. What do you say, Sarah?" Geoff asked with a smirk, starting to comprehend Sam's concern.

"I think that sounds like fun, Geoff. What time do you want to pick me up?" Sarah was oblivious to Sam's irritation.

"I said she can't go, Geoff...she's busy. She has to go with me to recruit floats for the parade." Sam struggled to think. "Yeah…so…ah… we'll be busy all day long. Sorry, Sarah, I just hadn't gotten around to calling you on that. We have a deadline on this and we need to get started right away and Saturdays are the best day because all the businesses in town are open." *Quick thinking Ward, quick thinking.*

"Oh, I'm sorry, Geoff. I didn't realize this. Maybe some other time." Sarah was quite flattered with all the attention she was getting but noticed Sam getting irritable and wondered if she was intruding on his 'guy's night out'.

"Will you gentlemen excuse me while I go to the ladies room?"

"Watching Sarah leave, Geoff glared at Sam. "What the hell's your problem? Do you have an issue with me asking Sarah out, although I don't know why you should have?" Geoff suspected this was the problem. "Well too damn bad. You've had your chance with her."

"You're an asshole, Geoff. The last person I would ask out is Sarah. She's A.J.'s sister-in-law. He'd kill me if I asked her out but I can assure you that you're not going to either." Sam was getting angry.

"Whoa Boys, settle down. Who wants another beer? I'm buying." Rudy tried to ease the tension between the two men.

Geoff grew defensive. "Who gave you protection rights? She's a big girl and can make her own decis..." Geoff stopped mid-sentence as Sarah returned to the seat beside him.

"Wow, interesting washrooms, they have beagles everywhere in there. Anyway guys it was nice to meet you all but I need to find my sister and A.J. We are going to the drive-in tonight and I'm sure I must have misunderstood where to meet them. Take care, Sam. I'll see you on Saturday and thanks again for the drink, Geoff."

Standing up Geoff turned on the charm. "My pleasure pretty lady." Giving Sam a snide look, Geoff smiled and asked, "Hey Sarah, since Sam has made it clear that Saturday is out, why don't we make it Sunday instead, nine o'clock too early?" And with his hand behind his back, out of Sarah's sight, Geoff flipped his middle finger at Sam. *Two can play at this game, Sammy Boy,* Geoff chuckled to himself.

CHAPTER EIGHTEEN

"Okay. Nine o'clock works great, Geoff, I'm looking forward to it."

Knowing Sam was angry Geoff decided he should get out while the going was good. "Wait up, Sarah, let me walk you to your car. Well Boys, I'm outta here. Here's my money and I'll see you on night shift."

Purposely trying to irritate Sam, Geoff leaned in and whispered in his ear, "Don't keep Sarah up too late working buddy, I wouldn't want her too tired for our big day on Sunday." And with that, Geoff winked at Sam and left with Sarah.

Asshole, thought Sam and saying good-bye to the rest of the guys, belted back the last of his beer and left. He was in a foul mood. *How the hell could Sarah agree to go out with Geoff? He's not even her type. Besides she's not going to have time to be dating Geoff, we have float recruiting to do.* Then the light bulb went on in Sam's mind and he smiled. *Oh I know how to fix this problem.*

NINETEEN

SATURDAY ARRIVED AND SARAH WAS looking forward to getting together with Sam and start recruiting floats. Getting dressed, she felt hungry. Hearing the phone ring, Sarah ran to the kitchen to answer it.

"Hello?'

"Sarah, it's Sam."

"Hi Sam, I'm almost ready to go. Where did you want to meet?"

"Well actually, Sarah, I forgot that I have some work to do at my place cleaning out my barn before the farmer who rents my property cuts the hay. He uses the barn to store hay for the winter and I need to get it done before next week. Do you think we could meet tomorrow instead?"

"Oh, sure we can although I was going to meet with Geoff tomorrow. But…I thought you said all the stores in town were closed on Sunday." Sarah wasn't sure what to do. Although she had been really looking forward to going out with Geoff she had made a commitment to Sam first and felt that was her priority.

"Oh yeah, right…I forgot about your date with Geoff. Well, I wouldn't want to interrupt that so we could meet another day next week...although, I did commit to getting this all done as quickly as possible. I suppose a few more days won't make too much of a difference and hopefully it won't throw off the schedule too much..." Sam was being manipulative and knew it. He purposely avoided the stores closing on Sunday scenario because quite frankly he didn't have an answer for that.

"No that's okay, Sam, I'm sure Geoff will understand."

Oh he'll understand all right. All too well I'm sure, he smiled.

"Are you sure, Sarah, because I know you were looking forward to going?" Sam tried to sound sincere.

"Oh absolutely, Sam, I committed to you first and Geoff and I can try for another day. I will give him a call right now to cancel and will see you tomorrow then. Where are we going to meet?"

"I'll pick you up around nine o'clock." And with that they said their goodbyes. Sam had to admit, he was rather satisfied with his performance.

That little bastard! Two can play at this game, thought Geoff as he listened to Sarah deliver the unexpected message. "Hey listen, Sarah, it's okay I'm sure Sam wouldn't have rescheduled if he really didn't have to." *The hell he wouldn't.*

"Listen, as it turns out I'm free today. Would you like to grab some lunch? I could take you out to Wallace Point and we can do some hiking? Are you up for that?"

"Sounds great to me, Geoff. I would love to go." Sarah was happy she didn't have to disappoint Geoff and the truth was she really wanted to spend some time with him. He seemed really nice and who wouldn't want to spend the day with a good-looking guy. His blond hair and brown eyes were rather captivating.

"Great. I'll pick you up at noon. See you then." Hanging up the phone, Geoff smiled. *Take that Sammy boy.*

After driving for what seemed like an hour Geoff finally pulled up to a bluff overlooking the valley. Getting out of the car Sarah was chilly and shivered. Looking around she was awestruck. "It's so beautiful here, Geoff. You can see for miles." Sarah stood at the railing overlooking Stone Valley. Far below she saw Forestville looking so small and peaceful against the beautiful fall backdrop. With the trees almost all changed to their fall colours it made for a stunning view. Sarah was speechless.

"This is where I always went hiking as a kid with my dad. It was where we spent our one-on-one time. I miss that."

"Did your dad move away?"

"No, he died when I was eleven years old. I rarely come back here but when I do I think about him and the times we spent here."

Sarah looked up at Geoff staring out over the valley deep in thought. In the distance she heard the sound of an eagle's screams. "I'm sorry to hear about your dad. It must have been difficult losing him at such a young age. Does your mom still live in Forestville?"

"No, she left shortly after Dad died and left me in the hands of my grandparents. I've never heard from her since. Of course my grandparents assured me that she loved me and naturally I always hoped she would come back, but in time I realized she wasn't going to and just gave up hope. Don't get me wrong; my grandparents did a great job raising me; my life has been awesome, but they weren't my mother, or my father for that matter. Needless to say, when my dad died they were devastated; he was their only son and they never really recovered from his death. They still live in Forestville but their age is showing and now I take care of them."

Sarah listened intently to what Geoff was saying. She was comfortable around him. A feeling she couldn't explain because she had just met him, but her instincts were guiding her and she was letting them. It just felt right. Standing in silence, Sarah was thinking of that eleven-year-old boy devastated by the loss of his father and then having his mother leave so suddenly. It had to have been heartbreaking. She felt surprisingly sad, not so much for Geoff, but for the boy who he once was.

Geoff interrupted the poignant moment. "Okay, so enough about this; let's eat. There's a nice little spot just down the path here that I think you will find is perfect for lunch."

They walked for about fifteen minutes. Sarah's mouth dropped open when they came upon an area that Geoff had obviously visited earlier. There were a couple of chairs, a blanket laid neatly on the ground and on it were plates, cutlery, wine glasses, a bottle of wine chilling in a bucket. As she watched, Geoff opened a small cooler and started pulling out a variety of cheeses, meats, fruit, baguette and to finish everything off, he placed a delicious looking homemade blueberry pie aside for afterwards. The piece de resistance was a small campfire he leaned in to light, taking the edge off the chilly day.

"Oh my God, Geoff, you're amazing. It's perfect. Thank you so much." Sarah was in awe of this big tough firefighter who was surprisingly sensitive and romantic; it was all completely unexpected but she was enjoying every moment. "No one has ever done something like this for me before. Thank you."

"I'm surprised, Sarah, because you're such a sweet, beautiful woman. Those other guys obviously didn't realize what they were missing."

CHAPTER NINETEEN

Oh boy is he charming, maybe a little too charming. Sarah was finding herself practically swooning with every word Geoff spoke. She was almost completely smitten and they hadn't even reached dessert yet.

"That son-of-a-bitch! I don't know what the hell he thinks he's doing!" Sam was angrier than he had been in a long time.

"Who's a son-of-a-bitch?" Bill asked.

Sam was standing in Bill's shop waiting to finally pick up his truck, not realizing that he was speaking out loud.

"Oh, ah, no one Bill." Sam tossed the Ford Taurus car keys onto the counter.

Bill wasn't one who liked to pry, but Sam was obviously upset about something. This surprised Bill because it was completely out of character for Sam to behave this way. For him to get this upset he must have been pushed pretty far.

"Who the hell does he think he is?" Sam practically tossed the money at Bill. "He bloody well knew what he was doing and purposely..."

"What the hell are yer talkin' about, Sam? What's got yer goat taday?"

"Geoff. I called his place and spoke to his grandmother. He knew I was supposed to work with Sarah today on the float recruitment and he took her out. Bastard!"

"So shouldn't yer be angry with Sarah instead? She knew she was supposed ta git that work done with yer so why in hell was she going with him?"

"No it isn't her fault, it's Geoff's."

"Doesn't sound that way ta me Sam."

"No, you don't understand. I was supposed to work with Sarah today so Geoff asked her out for Sunday. Then I told Sarah that I needed to get some work done today and we would have to work together tomorrow instead and so her date with Geoff would have to be cancelled."

"Okay, so what's the problem?" Bill was confused.

"So the bastard asked her out for today instead."

"Okay, so again, what's the problem?"

"Well she was supposed to be working with me today."

"Yeah, but yer cancelled that until tomorrow."

"Yeah because I told her I had work to do today and couldn't make it."

"So what's the problem?" Bill still wasn't following along at all. He was getting more confused by the minute.

"What do you mean what's the problem? The problem is that Geoff took Sarah out today instead of tomorrow and she was supposed to work with me today."

"But she can't work with yer taday because yer busy taday."

"Yeah but she wasn't supposed to go out with Geoff until tomorrow and she's gone with him today."

"That's great because now she can work with yer tomorrow...am I right?" Bill asked hesitantly.

"No that's not great Bill! That's not great at all! Oh the hell with it, you don't understand." Sam tried to end the conversation.

CHAPTER NINETEEN

Bill was quietly thinking when it suddenly occurred to him what was going on. Laughing, he offered, "Now I get it, Sammy boy. Yer jealous that Geoff is takin' Sarah out." Now it was all coming together in his mind.

Abruptly looking up at Bill the look on Sam's face could have frozen the hearts of the toughest of men.

"What the hell are you talking about, Bill? Of course I don't care if Geoff takes Sarah out! Why in hell would you say that?"

"Sammy, who are yer kidding my boy? Yer jealous!" Bill was grinning from ear to ear.

"You're an asshole, Bill!" Bill's words hit a nerve and Sam didn't like it. "What the hell are you talking about? I could care less who she dates! The woman is a complete disaster! Every time I'm around her I need to protect myself from getting physically hurt, she's one of the most infuriating people I have ever met not to mention short-tempered and unreasonable!"

"Don't think yer can fool me, Sammy!" It was all perfectly clear to Bill. Sam didn't show too much emotion over anything, but to see him this upset over a nice girl like Sarah pleased Bill. *Sam needs a good woman in his life. It's about time he settled down and quit dating the likes of Trish the dish. Them girls is trash and Sam deserves better than that.*

"Sarah can date whoever she wants. I'm just irritated because we were supposed to work together today that's all."

"Well I think yer full of shit. Man up for chrissakes and admit yer like the girl. The sooner yer admit it, the sooner yer can do something about it to win the girl over. But if all yer gonna do is whine and carry on like this then she's better off with a real man who fights fer what he wants. Now git yer sorry whiny ass outta my station and man the hell up."

Sam stood in shocked silence absorbing what Bill had just said.

Bill tossed the truck keys at Sam who fumbled to catch them and wondered, *What the hell's his problem?*

"Yer truck is done just like brand new, Sammy. Too bad a real man ain't driving that beauty."

Sam gave a look of dry sarcasm in Bill's direction.

"What the hell's your problem today anyway, Bill?" Sam shouted as he watched Bill walk off shaking his head in silence. Driving away, Sam was deep in thought. *Not sure what Bill's problem is today but I can assure you, Geoff my man, two can play at this game.*

TWENTY

THE NEXT DAY SAM PICKED up Sarah who presumed they were recruiting floats; but Sam had another idea.

"Sarah, there's been a change of plans today. The local animal shelter is short staffed and needs help with a new litter of pups they found abandoned. The mother was killed, they are too young to feed themselves and I wondered if you would mind giving me a hand?" *Who doesn't love puppies? Good luck topping this, Geoff my man! None of the stores in town are open today anyway and going to the shelter covers my ass on that.*

"Oh my God, that's so sad, Sam, and yes I would love to help. What a great idea." Sarah was delighted. She loved dogs and her heart broke at the thought of the pups losing their mother.

Arriving at the shelter, Sam greeted a young girl sitting at the front desk with familiarity. Surmising she must be in her mid-twenties Sarah couldn't help but notice her wide assortment of tattoos and piercings and choice of black clothing. *Wow this girl looks rather edgy for her young age.* It wasn't long though before Sarah was introduced to the softer side of this young lady.

"How's it going, Lisa? Come here and give me a big hug sweetheart!"

Sam was positively elated to see this young lady and was very sweet with her. Sarah was more curious than ever to figure out their connection.

"Sammy! I've missed you!" Lisa came around the desk and running towards Sam leaped into his arms straddling his body with a leg on either side of his waist. "Where've you been?"

Sam was laughing out loud at this point and gave the young girl a big hug and a kiss on the cheek. "I've missed you too. You look as beautiful as ever! I see you've changed your hair colour from pink to blue and it looks awesome on you! Is that a little more spike in your hair? I liked it the way it was but this makes you look even more beautiful!"

Hopping back down Lisa asked, "So where have you been, Sammy?"

"Well sweetheart, I've been busy taking care of some personal business that needed to be dealt with sooner rather than later."

With raised eyebrows Lisa asked, "Trish the dish? Did you finally kick that bitch out?"

Sam just smiled at the question. He didn't like to air his personal business in public but Lisa was remarkably intuitive.

"Well some relationships are better off ended." Sam grinned.

"I never liked her from the moment I met her when you adopted Benny. I'm glad you kicked her sorry ass to the curb, Sammy. You deserve better and I sure as hell hope you didn't let her keep Benny."

"Nope, Benny's with me so next time I come by I'll bring him in to see you. So Lisa, I would like to introduce you to a friend of mine. This is Sarah and she has graciously agreed to help with nursing some puppies."

"Hey." Lisa didn't make any qualms about the fact that she was visually interrogating Sarah. It made Sarah rather uncomfortable as she outstretched her hand to Lisa who didn't seem to notice.

CHAPTER TWENTY

"It's nice to meet you, Lisa, and I must say the colour of your hair is certainly eye-catching. Did Cathy colour it for you? I hear she's the best when it comes to hair colour." Sarah was rambling and knew it but Lisa was managing to make her feel ill at ease under her heavily 'mascara'd' stare.

Laughing Sam said, "Lisa, Sarah is a great person so take it easy on her."

"Yeah, okay." Lisa turned and started walking down the hall. "Come on, Sammy, the puppies are in 'B' wing in the big room. We were able to fit a space heater in there to keep them warm and cozy. You came at the perfect time, they are ready to be fed. C'mon."

Sarah dropped her hand back down to her side and self-consciously smiled at Sam who laughed and waved her on to follow them down the hall.

♡ ♡ ♡

"Sam's where?" Geoff wasn't happy about the news from Bill when he stopped by the station to get some gas for his truck.

"I said he's at the Westridge Animal Shelter. Thar's some pups that were abandoned and they needed help nursin' them. Why?" Bill knew the answer to the question but asked it anyway.

"No reason." Geoff was talking but his mind was planning his next move and it didn't take long for him to decide what to do. "Thanks, Bill, I'll see you later."

"Geoff! Git yer ass back here and pay fer the gas!" Bill was shaking his head as Geoff rushed back into the station and threw money on the counter and left.

He knew he shouldn't have told Geoff where Sam and Sarah had gone but he figured Sam needed a bit of a shake-up in his life and if he was going to get the girl, he needed to be pushed; he was being just a little too complacent as far as Bill was concerned. Placing the money in the till Bill shook his head and chuckled just thinking about how upset Sam was going to be when Geoff showed up. *Wish I could be a fly on that wall but I'm sure I'll be hearin' all about it.*

"Oh my God, Sam, they are absolutely adorable! What I wouldn't give to adopt one but I'm sure they're all spoken for by now."

Sarah sat on the floor with her back resting against the wall and knees bent, holding a golden retriever pup in her arms, feeding her a small bottle of warmed-up formula. The puppy was wrapped in a blanket and sucking so hard at the bottle that some of the formula was dripping out of her mouth and down her chin. Sarah had never felt so content in her life.

"Sam, I think it's so amazing that you volunteer like this. Thank you for bringing me here." Sarah finished feeding the one puppy and wiped its mouth clean then placed her back into the box and watched as she snuggled in with her siblings to get warm. Grabbing another puppy, Sarah looked up and found herself smiling as she watched how gentle Sam was feeding the pup he had. The look on his face was so peaceful and nurturing that Sarah couldn't take her eyes off of him. Suddenly he looked up at her. She felt embarrassed that he had caught her staring at him and looked away. She heard Sam chuckle and when she dared to look again he was trading the one pup off for another. *For such a big tough guy he seems to have such gentle hands. You are an interesting man Sam Ward. I can't help but wonder what life with you would be like.*

"This little one is my favourite of them all, Sam. She seems to be more blonde in colour than the others and she's smaller – almost seems like the runt of the litter." Sarah kissed the top of the little pup's head.

CHAPTER TWENTY

"I've always wanted another dog..." She became lost in her thoughts when suddenly she heard a familiar voice out in the hall and looking up saw Geoff being led into the room.

All that could be heard was Sam's shocked, "What the...?"

"Sam. Sarah. What are you doing here? I didn't know you would be volunteering here today. I thought you would be off recruiting floats." Geoff had a hard time hiding his sarcasm yet nothing made him happier than seeing the irritated look on Sam's face.

"What the hell brings you here, Geoff? I thought you hated dogs?" Sam almost spit the words out as he spoke.

"Me? Hate dogs? Not me buddy. You must have me mistaken for someone else. I love dogs."

Knowing Sarah wasn't looking, Sam gave Geoff the finger and with that Geoff laughed. *This is a game I have no intention of losing, Sammy boy!* Geoff then glanced in Sarah's direction.

"Here, let me help you with that." Reaching over and grabbing a bottle, Geoff handed it to her, then made himself comfortable on the floor forcing space between Sam and Sarah.

"Here Geoff, take this little one." Sarah laughed, watching Geoff awkwardly hold the puppy in mid-air. Have you ever fed a puppy this young before? Here, let me show you how to hold her." Taking the pup Sarah wrapped her in a blanket, showed Geoff what to do and then handed him a bottle to start feeding.

"Geoff, you look uncomfortable, are you sure you're okay?" Sarah chuckled at the sight of Geoff awkwardly shifting the puppy around while it squirmed and yelped, trying unsuccessfully to get food.

"Of course he doesn't know what the hell to do because he's never handled a dog a day in his life," Sam retorted snidely. "But he sure knows how to shovel shit and that's exactly what needs to get done once we finish feeding these puppies. The kennel needs to be cleaned out before we leave, Geoff, so you arrived at the right time."

Geoff glanced in Sam's direction with only his eyes and if looks could kill Sam would have been six feet under. Sam got up and left the room without a word and with that Geoff jumped at his opportunity.

"So Sarah, I thought you and Sam were supposed to be recruiting floats today?" Geoff was trying not to sound irritated.

"Well, we were supposed to but plans changed and quite honestly I like this plan better." Sarah kissed the little pup she held in her arms and smiled, watching as it yawned and began to fall asleep now that it had a full tummy.

"I see..." Geoff was strategizing in his mind.

"Geoff, watch what you're doing. The pup can't even reach the bottle to eat." Sarah laughed at the sight of the little puppy's mouth trying to reach the nipple. Geoff rolled his eyes and roughly stuffed the nipple in and the puppy noisily suckled away.

"So, what plans do you have tonight?"

"Nothing really, why?" Sarah stared down at the content pup thinking how nice it would be to have a dog of her own to keep her company.

"I was wondering if you would like to go to dinner with me tonight. I thought we could go to the Old Beagle and grab some wings."

"Actually I'm treating Sarah to dinner tonight, Geoff." Neither heard Sam return and seeing the surprise on Sarah's face added, "As a thank you for helping me out here."

Really? Geoff thought sarcastically. *The hell you are.* "Where are you going? I'll join you."

CHAPTER TWENTY

"Well that would be impossible…I'm…well…" Sam was scrambling to think. "I'm actually cooking at my house tonight and I only have enough for two. Maybe some other time buddy."

The look on Geoff's face was almost visually saying, 'Touché'. Sam was rather pleased with himself.

After the pups were all fed they began cleaning up the dog pen. Sam felt gratified seeing the disgusted look on Geoff's face and thought it was almost worth the aggravation of having him show up today.

While Geoff was busy cleaning the kennel Sam and Sarah bathed each of the pups and dried them off before putting them into their bed. Sam smiled at the sight of Sarah carefully drying each puppy then kissing them on their heads before putting each one back.

"Shit!"

Sarah and Sam looked in Geoff's direction wondering what was going on.

"How could there be so much shit from such little animals? This is disgust…" Looking up and seeing Sam and Sarah staring with eyebrows raised in his direction Geoff quickly regrouped. "I mean, it really is no trouble cleaning it up, I'm just amazed that such cute little fur balls could eliminate so much!" Realizing he almost slipped up, Geoff chuckled to lighten the mood and added, "They are very cute though aren't they?" *Christ I hate dogs!*

As they were about to leave the shelter, Geoff was trying to get Sarah alone in the hall while Sam locked up the kennel where the puppies were. "Sarah, can I talk to you for a moment?"

"Sure Geoff, what's up?"

"Oh Mr. Linton, I've been looking for you."

Lisa seemed to appear out of nowhere and approached Geoff with obvious intent.

"Mr. Linton, I was wondering if I could get you to assist me with another kennel that has a few adult dogs in it. Since you said you are comfortable with dogs I could really use your help walking each one in our compound. It won't take you long. I promise. We are really short-staffed and…here, come this way and let me show you." Lisa grabbed Geoff by the arm and dragged him reluctantly down the hall with her. Looking back, Lisa knowingly winked at Sam.

Sarah was confused because Geoff didn't seem at all like he knew Lisa and yet he said he had been here many times before. Waving to Geoff as he left Sarah yelled after him, "Call me tomorrow."

"Okay Sarah, let's get going." Sam quickly ushered her out the front door. "Nice of Geoff to offer to help Lisa like that," Sam said sheepishly, knowing full well that it wasn't Geoff who had volunteered his services at all. *The bastard hates dogs with a passion. I must remember to bring Lisa some flowers for helping me out.*

TWENTY-ONE

SITTING IN SAM'S KITCHEN, SARAH sipped on the wine he had poured her. "Sam, I had so much fun at the shelter today. Those pups were absolutely adorable and I'm sure they will be adopted in no time at all." Taking another sip of wine she was feeling more relaxed than she likely should have been. "Thanks again for taking me to get my car. I need to head out fairly soon after dinner because I have a few things to get done at home."

"Sure, no problem."

"Can I help you chop those vegetables? I feel like I'm being rude just sitting here while you do all the cooking."

"Got it all under control. My mother didn't raise a slouch when it came to cooking. Well actually, my dad could cook up a storm although most of his cooking was limited to the BBQ but you'd be hard pressed to make a better steak than my father did." Sam smiled at the fond memory.

"You didn't have to do this Sam. I would have helped you today without a meal but I must admit, the more I smell that pork tenderloin cooking the hungrier I get. What did you marinade it in? It smells divine." Sarah leaned over from the far side of the island counter to get a closer whiff of the leftover marinade.

"Ah, but that's a family secret. If I told you I'd have to kill you." Sam winked at Sarah, grinned and continued with the cooking.

"Don't you ever get lonely out here all by yourself? Don't get me wrong; it's nice here but you seem to be a really social guy."

Thinking for a minute Sam answered, "I do get lonely, sometimes, but usually this is my escape from the craziness of the world out there. I prefer to have some thinking time and I can't do that anywhere else. What about you though? You're all by yourself at the lake. Don't you ever get lonely?"

"Yes, I definitely do, but I'm close enough to town that I can go see Terri and A.J. whenever I want and…well…it's a bit of an escape… water is my solace, always has been." Sarah was thoughtful for a moment and poured herself more wine. Sighing contentedly, she sat back down on the couch. Tucking her feet up under herself, she hugged a pillow and stared off into space thinking about nothing in particular. She could hear the crickets outside although they weren't as plentiful as they had been in the summer, they still hung in there, possibly in the hopes that winter would never come. "It really is peaceful here. I feel very comfortable. Strange really, I can't explain it," she said quietly to no one in particular.

"Dinner will be ready shortly. Would you like more wine with dinner?"

"Sure, why not!"

Dinner was delicious. Sarah couldn't remember a time when she felt more relaxed albeit the wine she had been drinking certainly helped with that. She couldn't pinpoint why, but Sam made her feel…well…he made her feel…safe. *What is it about this man? He brings out the worst and the*

best in me. He can infuriate me, yet put a smile on my face. Oh boy Sarah, how many men do you need in your life? You just kicked Travis to the curb and now Sam and Geoff seem to be complicating things.

As the evening progressed, Sarah ended up pouring herself several glasses of wine and found herself giggling from the effects.

"You know, Sam. I didn't like you very much when I first met you." Sarah knew she was actually starting to slur her words a bit but couldn't stop herself from uttering out loud what she was thinking. It was like she had taken a truth serum.

Sam chuckled. *This girl is going to have one nasty headache in the morning if she keeps drinking that wine.*

"I think you've had enough wine Sarah. I'll make you some coffee." When Sam got up to put the coffee on Sarah jumped up and stood in front of him, looking up and wobbling slightly as she stared intently into his eyes. Sam could see that Sarah's eyes were glazed over from the wine.

"Sam…"

Sam waited but she said nothing. Smiling he went to step around her but she moved and blocked his way.

"Wait! Sam! I have to tell you…I have to tell you that…you have the 'blueist' blue eyes I've ever seen. Has anyone ever told you that?" Sarah swayed. "Yup. Yup, you really do." Clear thinking was becoming a strain for Sarah.

"You weren't very nice to me when we first met. I did not like you very much. Did you know that? Nope. I didn't."

"I think you've had enough wine, Sarah." Sam hadn't kept track but looking over at the kitchen counter he realized that there were two empty wine bottles and he had only two glasses all evening. *Now I understand. Okay, so no driving home for this girl.* Smiling, Sam guided

Sarah by the shoulders and directed her to the couch giving her a slight push to sit down. Sarah cooperated.

"You know, Sam. I didn't like you very much. Did I tell you that?"

"Yes you did, Sarah...several times as a matter of fact." Sam admitted her honesty was getting a bit irritating and went to start coffee. *Good thing I'm not easily offended,* he chuckled to himself.

"But you know what, Sam?"

"What Sarah?"

"I like you, now. I like you a lot now." Nodding her head, Sarah closed her eyes for a few seconds.

"Well I'm glad. Thank you. I like you too." Sam was chuckling out loud as he made the coffee. He could feel Sarah staring at him the entire time. When the coffee was finally made he poured a cup, took it over to her and placed it on the coffee table. It was then that Sarah grabbed Sam by the sleeve pulling him down beside her.

"Sam. How come you weren't very nice to me when we met? I'm a nice person." Sarah paused almost as if she was straining to think. "You weren't nice at all to me...why?"

"Yes, you are a nice person, Sarah, and I'm sorry about that. Here, drink your coffee." Sam put the cup of coffee into Sarah's hands and helped guide her with the first sip.

Shaking her head, Sarah carelessly put the cup back down onto the table splashing it all over. When Sam was about to stand up she lunged at him and planted a big ole wet drunken kiss onto his lips sending him backwards onto the couch. Admittedly, he was taken aback at first but once they were past the awkwardness, he started kissing her in return, gently at first and then more passionately. Sliding his right hand up into her hair Sam placed his left hand on her back, gently pressing her closer to him. Sarah's kisses were passionate and intense and Sam responded. Reaching for Sam's shirt Sarah began to unbutton each button one by one. It was then that Sam realized he couldn't do this.

"Sarah, stop. Stop. I won't do this." Gently pushing her off of him Sam sat up and started to button his shirt back up.

"Why Sam? What's wrong?" Sarah was drunk but understood what was happening.

"Sarah, I can't do this. You've had too much to drink; it's not right; I won't do it. Another time when you haven't had so much to drink, if you feel the same way then I'm game because let me tell you, it's just about killing me not to make passionate love to you. But I won't; not now; not this way…not tonight, Sarah." All Sam wanted at that moment was a cold shower but instead he got up and poured himself a coffee. Looking over at Sarah, she looked hurt but hadn't said a word.

As much as Sam regretted his decision, he knew it was the right thing to do. He wouldn't take advantage of this situation. If it was truly meant to happen between him and Sarah and not just in a drunken stupor then he wanted the moment to be perfect, not like this. "It's late, Sarah. I'll finish putting the food away and then I'll drive you home."

Cleaning up Sam knew it had become very quiet and initially thought Sarah was upset with him until he looked over to see that she had fallen asleep sitting up, hugging a pillow. Walking over and standing beside the couch Sam looked down at her sleeping. He smiled at the sound of her loud snoring, the tussled hair all over her face and the drool coming out of her mouth. He knew that she would regret the hangover she was sure to have in the morning. Adjusting her so she was lying down Sam covered Sarah up with a blanket, kissed her on the forehead, turned the lights off and headed to bed.

TWENTY-TWO

THE NEXT MORNING SARAH AWOKE to the sun shining on her face and a vicious headache. It took her a few minutes to comprehend that she was still at Sam's place. *Oh my God. What have I done?* Before she could open her eyes to the bright day she covered her head with the blanket until she adjusted to the daylight. Putting her hand onto her forehead Sarah moaned realizing that this was going to be a long, rough day. Sitting up she noticed she was still dressed and her mouth was really dry. *Oh boy. Red wine doesn't agree with me.*

Heading to the washroom Sarah shut the door and started scouring Sam's cabinet looking for some sort of headache medicine. Finally finding it she decided to grab three pills instead of two. *This definitely calls for a little extra today.* Not even looking in the mirror, Sarah walked back into the kitchen searching for a water glass but her head was pounding so much that she had to sit down at the kitchen table. Putting her head down she closed her eyes for a few moments. *What the hell was I thinking last night? In fact, I don't even think I can remember most of last night. Oh boy, that can't be good. Oh my God, my stomach isn't doing so well either.*

Running back to the washroom, Sarah shut the door and promptly threw up in the toilet. Once finished she sat on the floor, leaned her head back against the wall and closed her eyes. *I am so embarrassed. What will Sam think? Oh boy, here I go again...* Several minutes went by but Sarah finally got it all out of her system. Finally, feeling it was safe to leave the washroom, she rinsed with some mouthwash she found in Sam's cabinet, walked back into the kitchen and was mortified to see that Sam was up making coffee.

"Well, good morning, Sunshine. How're you feeling?" Sam grinned at the sight of her. She was a mess.

Sitting down at the table, Sarah rested her head face down on her arms and closed her eyes.

"Not good I see." Sam was greatly amused but sympathized. He had been in the same position many times in the past and it wasn't fun. "Can I get you a coffee or something to eat?"

"No! No food!" Sarah practically moaned at the thought.

"You know if you eat some food you will likely feel better but first you need to hydrate. Here's some water. Drink up." Sam purposely banged the glass of water loudly down onto the table right by Sarah's head.

Startled, she jumped and lifted her head just enough to see where the glass was. Taking the acetaminophen she found, she drank all the water in the glass and then dropped her head back down.

"I have to go lie down again." Sarah stumbled back to the couch, covered herself up and promptly fell back to sleep.

Opening her eyes once more Sarah was surprised to see the sun was setting and that she was still at Sam's place. Her legs felt cramped and it was only then she realized Benny had been sleeping with her on the couch. Seeing that Sarah was awake Benny hopped off and started licking her face making her laugh out loud.

"Okay, okay Benny, that's enough." Patting him Sarah sat up and tossed the blanket aside. *Oh boy I was in worse shape than I thought. Thank God I feel better but now I'm starving.* As soon as she vacated the couch Benny hopped back up making himself comfortable once more. Wondering where Sam was, Sarah noticed a note on the counter for her.

Sarah,

I didn't want to wake you up.
There's some dinner in the microwave for you.
I'll be back shortly.

Sam
P.S. Don't worry, your snoring didn't disturb me.

Sarah cringed at that last part. "Oh my God, I'm so embarrassed."

"Well, just because you snore like a sailor and drool like ole Benny here is no reason for you to be embarrassed."

Sarah hadn't noticed Sam standing there and rolled her eyes at the comment.

"How long did I sleep?"

"Well, suffice to say that you've lost a whole day and other than waking up briefly this morning to throw up and grab something for your headache, you pretty much slept the better part of seventeen hours."

Sarah groaned, "I'm so sorry, Sam. I can't believe I drank so much. I hope I behaved myself. I can't really remember much after we had dinner." Sarah was apprehensive about the answer.

Hesitating, Sam was trying to decide whether to let her know the truth or allow her to avoid the humiliation of the events from the night before.

"You were fine. Nothing to worry about."

"Oh, thank goodness for that." Sarah was relieved.

"Here, why don't you go wash up and let me warm up some dinner for you. You must be starving."

Sarah went to the washroom to freshen up and looking into the bathroom mirror her mouth dropped open.

"Oh my God! My hair's a mess, my eye makeup's smudged…I look like the local whore who just wrapped up her night. All that's missing is the red light over the door."

Sarah was mortified at the thought. Finding a washcloth, she washed her face and found a comb to fix her hair as best she could. Searching through Sam's cabinet she found a new toothbrush to use and brushed her teeth. Feeling much better she walked back out to the kitchen.

"I see you found a washcloth and comb." Sam chuckled.

Rolling her eyes Sarah ignored him and sat down at the table to the plate of food Sam had placed there for her. After eating leftover pork tenderloin and a salad, Sarah felt almost one hundred percent albeit a little worn out.

"Thanks, Sam. You've been so gracious. I just can't believe that I did that. I haven't had that much to drink in a long time. Well except when Travis and I broke up..."

"Don't worry about it. Ole Benny here enjoyed having someone to share the couch with. He slept with you all night long. He wouldn't leave you."

CHAPTER TWENTY-TWO

Looking over at Benny, Sarah smiled seeing the dog stretched fully across the couch taking up almost every inch of space available.

"Are you sure, Sam? It seems to me that he may have resented having to actually share the couch." Sarah laughed. "Well, I guess I should leave so you can have your home to yourself. Thanks again, yesterday at the shelter was amazing…" Thinking for a moment Sarah asked, "It was yesterday, right?"

Laughing, Sam offered, "Yes it was yesterday and I'm glad you enjoyed yourself but you don't have to leave just yet, Sarah. You are welcome to stay. It's nice having some company for a change. Why don't you have a cup of peppermint tea to help keep your stomach settled before you leave."

Sam put the kettle on and Sarah wandered over to pat Benny. It was comfortable here at Sam's, it was almost as if she belonged here. Looking around the kitchen and watching Sam make tea, Sarah felt like… well…she felt like she was at home. She was sad at the thought of leaving. Truth be told, she really didn't want to go but knew she shouldn't over stay her welcome. Looking up at Sam, who looked up at her at the same time, they stared knowingly at each other. No words were spoken but they knew.

Sam turned the stove off, walked around the counter towards Sarah who stood up and walked towards him. Falling into each other's arms they passionately kissed knowing this was what they both wanted.

TWENTY-THREE

Sarah awoke the next morning lying in Sam's arms, feeling happier and more content than she had ever felt before. Smiling to herself she reflected on the night before, which had been filled with passionate lovemaking and very little discussion. Sam was a very gentle lover, more so than Travis who was far too selfish to be a good lover. Sarah had never felt this way with Travis.

Turning onto her side towards Sam, Sarah watched him sleep and smiled contentedly. *He looks so peaceful.* Reaching out she used her index finger to gently push hair off his face. *This is the way it should always feel. The way I should always feel.* Sighing out loud, she closed her eyes once again and drifted off to sleep.

Sarah was dreaming. She was lying on a dock with Sam beside her, relaxing in the warm sun and listening to the water lap against the shoreline. She could hear Sam calling her from a distance, which was strange since he was lying right beside her.

"Sarah? Sarah! Wake up sleepy head. I would have thought you got enough sleep after your drunken soiree in my kitchen."

When she finally opened her eyes she realized she was still in his bed, naked and cozy under the sheets with Sam standing beside the bed looking at her. He was dressed, with a coffee in his hand and grinning.

All Sarah could do was smile back then close her eyes again. She was sleepy and comfortable and didn't want to wake up nor did she want to get out of Sam's cozy warm bed. She wanted to say out loud, 'Go away, Sam. I want to stay here forever. I don't want it to end', but all she could muster was, a sleepy, "What time is it?"

Eventually dragging herself out of bed, Sarah grabbed Sam's housecoat and walked down the hall where she could hear him working in the kitchen. Benny had been sleeping on the couch and when he heard Sarah he ran down the hall to greet her. Kneeling down, she laughed as he licked her face.

"Benny! Come!" Sam shouted from the kitchen.

Obediently Benny ran to Sam and was generously rewarded with a dog treat and then sent outside.

Shivering, Sarah crossed her arms tightly in front of her and trundled into the kitchen in her sock feet and leaned over the stove to see what Sam was preparing.

Before she could say a word Sam wrapped his arms around her and pulled her tightly against his body. "Good morning. I trust you slept well."

Sarah closed her eyes. *Oh my God all I want to do is rip your clothes off Sam Ward.* She had to catch her breath as Sam kissed her forehead, her cheek and then softly pressed his lips against hers and kissed her gently at first and then with determination. Sarah wrapped her arms around him bringing him closer. She could feel him opening the robe exposing her breasts to his gentle caress. Holding her breath she felt Sam's fingers gently work their way around her nipples; she moaned with pleasure. Sam then removed his lips from hers and leaning down began to suckle her nipples to the point where Sarah felt like she was melting from the touch of his tongue. Licking her own lips Sarah's head slowly fell backwards as she allowed Sam to move from her nipples to her stomach and slowly downward. Sarah's legs were weakening by the second. Slowly helping her lay down onto the floor, Sam sensuously used his fingers to massage between her legs until she almost reached climax and then slowly slid into her. Sarah held her breath momentarily. Sam began suckling her nipples once again and it wasn't long before she could hear herself moaning out loud with climactic pleasure, followed by Sam's response inside of her and his moaning approval. Enjoying the aftermath of their passion, Sam and Sarah were silent, laying side by side and enjoying the moment when suddenly they heard…

"Sammy, darling? Are you home? Well you must be, there's a car in your driveway so I know you have company."

"Oh shit!" Sam whispered in Sarah's ear as he scrambled to sit up and hide behind the counter. Grabbing his pants and frantically pulling them on, Sam peeked around the corner of the counter. "What's *she* doing here?"

"Who?" Sarah quickly wrapped the robe around her and tied up the belt. Sitting up she fussed with her hair trying to make it more presentable. *Because of course, that would help make everything better,* she thought feeling ridiculous.

"Stay here!" Sam whispered.

"What? Why?" Sarah was confused until she heard the voice once again.

"Sam honey, where are you?"

Trish! Oh my God it's Trish! I can't let her see me here…like this…with Sam! Sarah was starting to panic and crawling on her hands and knees headed down the hall towards the washroom, tripping over the housecoat as it dragged along with her. *This is ridiculous! What the heck am I doing crawling on the floor hiding?* Sarah couldn't believe it and yet felt relief that she couldn't be seen from the front door. From the kitchen she could hear Sam talking.

"Trish. Why are you here and why are you just walking into my house like this?" Sam was completely unimpressed. *I need to get the locks changed.*

"Why were you on the floor?" she curiously asked.

"What do you want Trish?" Sam asked impatiently.

And that was the last Sarah heard before finding her clothes in Sam's room to get dressed. *I gotta get outta here before Trish sees me. I don't want the whole town knowing about this.*

Even though her intention had been to walk out to the kitchen as if nothing was wrong, Sarah's judgement was clouded and she assumed that if she did, Trish would never believe that nothing had happened. The whole town would know what went on. Sarah didn't want that. *No, no, no. That would be way too much to deal with.* So she decided to make quick her escape through the sliding glass door in the guest room, get to her car and leave before Trish even knew she was there. *So much for leaving on a romantic note*, she thought with dismay.

Quickly getting dressed, Sarah found herself sneaking out the guest room door like she had just robbed the place, tiptoeing around the house and out to the driveway with her purse tucked snuggly under her arm. Keys in hand, she reached her car and felt relief. *Time to get the hell out of here. Could this get any more embarrassing?* Just as she unlocked the car door, she received the answer to her question.

"Just as I thought honey. It was you Sam was fucking. I thought I recognized that car from the last time we met here."

Sarah dropped her head forward, let out a sigh and thought, *Yup, it sure could.* Hesitantly she turned around to look at Trish smiling rather sheepishly.

CHAPTER TWENTY-THREE

"Oh hey, Trish. What a surprise to see you here." *Really Sarah? That's all you've got?*

Trish stood with one knee bent, staring at Sarah, holding a lime green clutch purse in her left hand with her other hand sitting snuggly on her right hip.

"Somehow it doesn't surprise me..." Rather uninterested Trish added, "...that Sam decided to bed you honey. You are kinda cute...well, in a wholesome, plain sort of way, if that's what you're into."

Sarah felt Trish was looking rather 'bright' for a fall day. She wore a flashy floral, very snug-fitting top that showed so much cleavage even Sarah had to force herself not to stare. She also had on a bright yellow car coat, fuchsia skinny jeans, spiked heels and large hoop earrings. Her shoulder-length hair was tatted high up on her head and her bright red lipstick completed her heavily made-up look. Her entire image was reminiscent of a fifties Hollywood look, even the gum chewing seemed to fit in with the ensemble.

"...of course...I'm a hard act to follow," Trish continued between chews.

Sarah had been so transfixed by Trish's outfit that she had missed part of the conversation.

"Oh Sam didn't 'bed' me Trish. No, no, why would you think that? No...I was...um...I was...just visiting...discussing something with him about the, ah...about the...parade! Yes! The parade. Actually I was just leaving. Sam was too busy to...um...talk." Sarah knew she was stuttering with her words but couldn't stop herself.

Looking rather bored with the whole situation, Trish blankly stared at Sarah watching with amusement as she tried to explain herself.

"Oh I'm certain he was too busy to 'talk' honey but it seems to me that you managed to deliver your message rather nicely just the same."

Indignant, Sarah thought, *What the hell does that mean? Come on Sarah think of something to say. You're a grown woman with nothing to be embarrassed about. This isn't high school. Get it together girl!*

"So Trish. You look rather…" clearing her throat Sarah added, "… nice today." Feeling overwhelmingly uncomfortable, Sarah tried to stand tall and proud. She reached one hand out to lean up against her car but managed to miss it and almost fell trying to catch her balance once again.

Watching with knowing pleasure, Trish snickered and saying nothing walked to her car. As she opened the driver's door, she stopped and thinking for a moment offered, "I'm done with him now honey. He's all yours. You're more than welcome to my sloppy seconds." She practically snorted the words out with disgust, got into her car and skidded her way down the driveway.

"Oh my God. That was humiliating! What the hell were you thinking, Sarah? 'You look rather nice?' What was that?" Sarah chastised herself. "I have to get out of here." Getting in her car she couldn't leave fast enough. As she drove home Sarah realized why her story had no credibility with Trish when she noticed her shirt was inside out and the buttons misaligned. *Oh that's just the icing on the cake*, she relented.

TWENTY-FOUR

THROUGHOUT THAT AFTERNOON, SARAH KEPT lamenting over what had taken place with Trish and was too embarrassed to answer the phone the many times Sam had tried calling her since she arrived home. And as if that wasn't bad enough, Geoff had also left several messages for her to call. She was confused and needed time to think over what had taken place the last couple of days.

After dinner she put on a fire in the fireplace, grabbed a bottle of wine and just sat down in the living room when the telephone rang again. Leaving it to go to message she fully expected it to be Sam or Geoff but finally deciding to check, she stopped cold when she heard Travis' familiar voice.

"Baby, what are you doing cheating on me? How could you fuck another guy like that when I still love you Sarah?" She could tell he was drunk. "I'll be coming to see you real soon, Baby. You still have to pay for wrecking my car and if I were you, I'd stay away from that fire boy Sarah or I'll have to teach him a lesson for fucking my girl." Shaking and numb Sarah clumsily hung up the phone. This was all too much for her to deal with right now. She needed time to think. Think about what took place with Sam. Time to think about Geoff. Time to think about the humiliating moment with Trish and especially time to figure out what to do about Travis. *It's ridiculous involving A.J. over this. Travis would never hurt me. I know he's just trying to frighten me.* She was having difficulty trying to convince herself of this fact though, so, after double-checking that all her doors and windows were locked, Sarah decided to bring her baseball bat up from the basement and placed it beside her reclining chair, just in case. Having a glass or two of wine to calm down, Sarah slowly began to relax. She had consciously decided to drink her evening away, but that plan fell through when after a few glasses she fell asleep in the chair.

Startled awake, Sarah opened her eyes to the realization that someone was standing at the end of the chair staring at her. It had turned dark out and there were no lights on in the living room. Still groggy, she feared it was Travis and brought her foot up good and hard, kicked him in the groin and pushed him down so she could get away. *Thank you Daddy for teaching me that move.*

Crumbling to the floor, he moaned in agony. Sarah then managed to jump to her feet, grab the bat and holding it over her head screamed, "Don't move or I'll slug you!" Cautiously she backed up to turn the lamp on and doing so immediately dropped the bat to the floor and ran over to her attacker.

"Oh my God, Sam! I'm so sorry! I didn't realize it was you!" Sam couldn't say anything as Sarah helped him up to the couch.

It was several minutes before he could bring himself to speak but when he finally found his voice Sam asked, "Are you purposely trying to kill me because if you are I can certainly think of a lot less painful ways of going about it." Sam was sitting back on the couch with his eyes closed, deep in concentration trying to ride the wave of pain he was experiencing.

CHAPTER TWENTY-FOUR

"I'm so sorry Sam. I was startled. It was dark..." Then fully comprehending what had just taken place, Sarah added, "How could you! You practically scared me to death!"

"You've got to be kidding me? After kicking me like a mule in the groin that's what you have to say?" Sam moaned.

Cringing, Sarah asked, "Do you want...um...an ice pack or something?" She wasn't quite sure what to offer him considering where he was hurt.

"No, I don't want an ice pack!" Sam could barely get the words out.

"Can I get you a drink?" Sarah was annoyed but she really did sympathize with him. *It's really gotta hurt.* She winced at the thought.

"Yes, I want a drink! Oh my God!" Bending over in pain, Sam added, "And some pain killers."

It took quite a while for the pain to subside although the alcohol helped take the edge off. Sarah just kept filling Sam's glass in the hopes that he would forgive her sooner than later. *Why does this always happen to me? Well, okay, to Sam.* Chuckling to herself, Sarah couldn't help but smile at the absurdity of the entire scenario.

"How did you get in? I locked all my doors." Sarah was curious.

"Not all of them. Your sunroom door was unlocked." Sam moaned.

"Why didn't you turn a light on in the living room?"

"I didn't want to wake you up" Sam was still having difficulty getting the words out. "Why didn't you answer any of my calls, Sarah? I was getting worried. By seven when I hadn't heard from you I decided to come here to see what was going on."

Biting her lip, Sarah wasn't quite sure what to say. "Oh my God, Sam...I was completely humiliated. I snuck out the guest room door and when I reached my car I was accosted by Trish." Sarah conveyed the entire story to Sam who shook his head at the thought of Trish confronting Sarah like that.

"Don't let Trish intimidate you. She's just upset with me and as much as I'm sure she took great pleasure in making you feel uncomfortable, she's so wrapped up in herself she wouldn't even think to talk to anyone about what happened. It would be too humiliating for her to admit that she was 'replaced' so quickly. Not that I look at it that way, but she would. Don't give her another thought." Sam tried to reassure Sarah but he could tell she wasn't convinced.

"I have to admit though, it was pretty funny to see you crawling down the hall on your hands and knees." Sam laughed in the hope that it would lighten the mood a bit.

"Yeah, well..." Sarah shifted uncomfortably on the couch. "What if she caught us...although, I suppose she did...sort of." Rolling her eyes Sarah wasn't sure how to feel about everything. She hadn't even had the time to come to terms with what had taken place between Sam and her.

"Well, if she caught us then she would have been witness to something she and I never had." Sam cautiously looked at Sarah and added, "Intimacy, respect and love."

Sarah stopped cold. *What? Did I hear him correctly? Did Sam just say 'love'?*

"What did you say?" Sarah was somewhat flabbergasted.

"I said 'love'. I love you Sarah."

Sarah just sat in stunned silence.

Just then the phone rang. *Saved by the bell.* She hated to admit it but she was relieved. It bought her more time to absorb what Sam had just divulged about his feelings towards her.

CHAPTER TWENTY-FOUR

Without even thinking she ran to answer the phone.

"Hello?" Sarah answered.

"Hello?" All she could hear at the other end was breathing. She knew it had to be Travis trying to scare her again and hung up quickly.

Seconds later the phone began ringing again and Sarah refused to answer this time.

"Are you going to pick that up? Sam asked.

"Um, no, yes, I suppose so." Picking up the phone her heart sank when she realized who it was.

"Oh, ah, hi Geoff." She really wasn't in the mood to speak to Geoff right now. Glancing over at Sam, Sarah had pleading eyes. She wanted this rollercoaster to stop but it didn't seem like it was going to anytime soon. Sam just smiled and leaned back thinking, *You lose ole boy. Better luck next time.*

"No, I'm fine Geoff. Just…busy. What's that? Go for dinner tomorrow night?"

Of course she won't go to dinner with you asshole!

"Dinner tomorrow night sounds great, Geoff. See you at the Old Beagle at seven. No, I'll meet you there. Yes, I'm sure it's fine. Bye Geoff."

Sam's mouth dropped open in shock.

"Are you seriously going to go out for dinner with him?" Sam was upset and couldn't contain his surprise.

"Yes I'm going for dinner with him. Do you think I'm going to leave him hanging? I need to talk to him. He's a nice guy Sam and I'm not going to tell him about us over the phone. Whatever 'us' is."

"What if I said I didn't want you to go?" Sam asked with caution.

"I would say that you have no say in the matter. It's about me, not you, Sam." Sarah 'dug her heels in' as they say and wasn't about to budge on the issue.

"And besides, we haven't even discussed the subject of 'us' yet. Did you say, what I thought you said? Love? Isn't that a little quick? You barely know me." Walking towards Sam, Sarah was cautious but feeling happier each step she took.

"Well, yes. I did say love." Sam smiled. *This girl is nothing but trouble for me but I'm hooked and there's no going back.*

"Sam, you have no idea what you would be getting into with me." Sarah's insecurities were rearing their ugly head.

"Oh, I think I know very well what I would be getting into with you, Sarah Roberts. These last couple of months and especially these last couple of days have been the best I have had in a very long time and it's because of you. You're bluntly honest, painfully stubborn, and frustratingly short-tempered and yet I can't get you off my mind. Why? Because you're independent, you challenge me. You're beautiful, sexy, and smart and the only woman who has ever managed to make me angry, cripple me with pain, and capture my heart all at the same time. I love you Sarah and I only hope you feel the same."

As he spoke, Sam stood up; cringing with the lasting effects of Sarah's kick; and walked towards her. Now standing right in front of her, he waited for her response.

"Well, Sam Ward, I must admit that I *am* dangerously attracted to you."

Leaning in towards Sarah, Sam kissed her and then slowly pulling away said, "Sarah."

"Yes Sam?"

"I'll take that ice pack now."

TWENTY-FIVE

SARAH AWOKE TO SAM'S WARM body lying beside hers and she smiled at the thought of him staying overnight. Closing her eyes, she sighed contentedly enjoying the moment for as long as possible before it was interrupted.

Almost as if on cue, the phone rang and Sarah figured if it was Travis, that she would 'fess' everything up to Sam and let him help her figure out how to deal with the situation. Cautiously she answered the phone, and then quietly squealed when she realized who it was.

"Chloe! Oh my God. I'm so happy to hear from you! How are you?" Not wanting to disturb Sam, Sarah jumped out of bed, threw her housecoat and slippers on, went to the living room and plopped down on the couch.

"Hey girlfriend! I'm doing great! I haven't heard from you in weeks and I was getting worried. Why haven't you called me?" Chloe was ecstatic to hear her friend's voice.

"Chloe, I have so much to tell you. Hey, are you going to come visit me one of these days? Can you get any time off?" Sarah had a wave of remorse that she lived so far from her best friend. She missed her terribly, even more now that she was talking with her.

"That's what I was calling about Sarah. I have two weeks off and wanted to come visit you."

Sarah squealed with joy like a little girl. "Yes, yes of course you can come. When can you be here?" Sarah could hardly wait to spend some time with her.

"Well, I was going to head up today if I could. Is that okay?"

"Of course it's okay, Chloe. I can hardly wait to see you." Sarah was overjoyed.

Hanging up the phone, she suddenly remembered she was to meet Geoff for dinner that night and wondered how she would work around that. As much as she hated to do it over the phone, Sarah decided to call Geoff and break the news to him about her and Sam.

♡ ♡ ♡

Hanging up from Geoff, Sarah was disappointed he hadn't taken the news harder.

"Well, that went better than expected. Not sure how to feel about that." He seemed less upset than she had expected and she wasn't sure why it bothered her so much but she didn't have time to think about that right now; she needed to get ready for Chloe's visit.

Sneaking quietly into the bedroom, Sarah crawled back under the covers and snuggled in with Sam. Hearing him snore, she smiled and after a few minutes kissed him lightly on the lips and left him to sleep while she showered and got dressed.

Sarah was beyond excited for her friend to come. The two girls had been friends since they were in elementary school and grew up doing everything together; they were inseparable. Chloe was always outrageously dressed with a different pair of eyeglasses from an eclectic collection she managed to accumulate and grow on over the years, one, that to this day, she was the proud owner of. Contrary to her outward appearance Chloe had always been the shy more reserved one of the two with Sarah being far more outspoken and tomboyish.

They were both somewhat of outsiders and never hung around with the 'it' crowd but they didn't care because they had each other and that was good enough for them. The majority of their time in high school was spent swooning over Barry Clement, captain of the football team, knowing full well that he never even noticed them let alone knew their names. But they didn't care because Barry was dreamy so they loved him from afar. They would sit in the bleachers beside the football field during practices, giggling and talking about what it would be like to date him, which they knew would never happen. They went to every football game and even went as far as following him home because he lived on the same street as Sarah.

When it came to prom, both Sarah and Chloe secretly hoped he would ask them but of course that was a pipedream that faded quickly. But no worries because the Sadie Hawkins dance was coming up. It seemed silly to have a Sadie Hawkins dance considering the times however it was 'the' retro dance of the year. Sarah and Chloe got excited just thinking about asking Barry.

Leading up to it they agreed that one of them would ask Barry and if he said, "No," then the other would ask him next. It was the perfect plan, however, their dreams were dashed when they heard that Lynda Watson already beat them to it and they were left wondering who to ask, knowing they could never be truly happy going with anyone other than Barry.

In the end, they didn't ask anyone nor did they even go to the dance. They stayed home and watched romantic comedy reruns, stuffing their faces with chips, dip and soda, wallowing in the knowledge that Barry was at that very moment dancing with Lynda. It was misery. Neither girl had a boyfriend during high school. They had lived through their ugly duckling years there and it wasn't until they were in university that they seemed to blossom. With Barry in the distant past they started dating others, none of which lasted very long for Sarah, until she met Travis.

Travis Boynton was the handsome and charming Grainger University's football team captain and their star quarterback. Sarah fell madly in love. She couldn't help it; she was a sucker for a football player. Focussing on her studies, Sarah eventually graduated Grainger U with her business degree and Travis did what he had to do to keep his grades up and still play football.

In his fourth year at Grainger and with only one-year left, Travis accepted an incredible opportunity in Watertown with the Broncos as their star quarterback and his golden ticket into professional football. There was no question, Travis decided to leave university and move to Watertown with Sarah following close behind, finishing her degree the year they left.

It was after moving to Watertown that Travis began to change. His ego got the best of him and he started treating Sarah like she wasn't important anymore. They had been dating for several years and Sarah was reluctant to walk away from the relationship until that fateful day when she found him with Gretchen and the rest of her story was history.

Sarah hadn't spoken much to Chloe since she moved to Forestville and was especially curious to find out how her love life was. Chloe's long-term relationship with Bernard Abbotsford had been fantastic until his parents got wind of it. She had met him working at the law firm of Percival, Talbot and Young where he was a promising up and coming attorney and she was a part-time law clerk. Unlike Chloe, Bernard came from a very wealthy family and as far as his parents were concerned, Chloe was beneath his social status. They managed to date for a number of years against the advice of Bernard's parents, however, it seemed that Chloe had been Bernard's forbidden fruit. When push came to shove he broke up with her to marry Sophia Young, the daughter of one of the partners, and Chloe was left to tend to her betrayed and broken heart. To this day Chloe hadn't been able to commit to anyone and lived the life of the free-spirited bachelorette, although Sarah knew she wasn't completely happy.

Shaking herself back to the task at hand, Sarah could hardly wait to tell Chloe all about Sam. The last time they saw each other had been the night they got drunk together at the local bar right before she left Travis. It was a night Sarah couldn't remember much about, but certainly remembered the horrible hangover that followed.

After Sam went home, Sarah managed to get most of her house in order before hearing a car door shut. Knowing who it was she ran to open the side door to let her friend in.

"Chloe!"

"Sarah!"

The two girls ran and hugged each other.

"I've missed you so much. Here, let me help you with your bags. Are those new glasses you have? They look great on you."

Heading into the house, Chloe and Sarah talked non-stop. "I have so much to tell you Chloe, I just don't know where to begin. Listen, it's almost dinner time and I thought we could head into town to eat and meet up with a friend of mine."

Chloe stopped and looked at Sarah with great interest.

"A friend? A male friend?" Chloe was hopeful. *Sarah deserves someone in her life that will treat her better than that jerk, Travis.*

Blushing, Sarah acknowledged her friend was indeed male.

"Chloe, I can hardly wait for you to meet Sam. He's such a great guy and nothing at all like Travis, thank God."

After showing Chloe around her place they headed into town to meet up with Sam. Sarah couldn't stop smiling at the thought of introducing him to her best friend. Just the thought of having him in her life made her realize that she was happier than ever.

Arriving at the Old Beagle, Sarah scanned the room and, finding Sam, guided Chloe over to the table where he was sitting near the bar.

Sam stood up to greet the ladies and although Sarah felt a little uncomfortable kissing him out in public, once she realized that no one was paying any attention anyway, relaxed.

"Sam, this is my best friend, Chloe. Chloe, this is Sam." Shaking hands, the two greeted each other and sat down. Sam waved the waitress over to take their drink order.

"So, Chloe, I hear you and Sarah have been friends since you were kids."

"Yes, that's right. I've known Sarah since elementary school. We've been through it all together." Laughing, Chloe looked at Sarah who was positively glowing. *She looks so happy. I never saw her smile like this with Travis.* "So, Sam, I hear you're a firefighter."

"Yes, I'm new as a full-timer. I've been a volunteer for the last five years, not sure that's saying much though. They tell me it helps but I still have a lot of learning ahead of me." Laughing, Sam thanked the waitress for bringing their drinks and they placed their food order.

The evening was spent with Chloe and Sarah telling Sam all about their misadventures growing up and Sam telling Chloe about all his misadventures with Sarah since they'd met. Chloe and Sarah were crying, they were laughing so hard listening to Sam's exaggerated version of what happened to him. Sam was comforted by the fact that he wasn't the only one who had fallen prey to Sarah's calamities.

Looking up, Sarah was surprised to see her sister and brother-in-law walk into the Old Beagle. Looking over, Terri and A.J. saw Sarah waving to them and walked over to join them at their table.

"Well, well here you are. We have been worried sick about you, Sarah. Where have you been the last couple of days?"

Sarah blushed at the thought of telling A.J. and Terri about her and Sam and tried to avoid the subject for as long as possible. "Terri, A.J., sit down. You remember Chloe don't you?"

"Hi, Chloe. When did you get into town? Oh my gosh, when was the last time we saw each other?" Terri sat down beside Chloe and promptly delved deep into conversation with her and completely forgot the fact that she hadn't seen or heard from Sarah the last few days.

"So, Sarah, where have you been? You haven't returned our messages. Your sister was getting worried. And Sam, you've been AWOL as well. What have you been up to? In fact, I don't think we've heard from either one of you since the weekend..."

A.J. suddenly stopped talking and just looked from Sarah to Sam and back again. The light bulb went on.

"No! Tell me it's not so."

"What A.J.? What's not so?" Terri suddenly caught wind of the other conversation and became curious as to what was being discussed.

Without even looking at Terri, A.J. pointed out, "These two. Is it true?"

Blushing, Sarah scrunched up her nose, feeling completely uncomfortable and Sam just grinned back at A.J. saying nothing for fear of a negative reaction.

"It is true. Oh my God, I can't believe it. You two? Really?" A.J. had been caught off guard but was realizing that it all made sense now.

"A.J., what are you rambling on about? What do you mean, these two?" Looking at Sarah and Sam, Terri suddenly realized what was going on and squealed with delight.

Sarah quietly nodded her head and Sam waited for A.J.'s reaction before getting too comfortable.

"Well, I think it's about bloody time. I think you were the only two who couldn't see this happening." A.J. flagged the waitress down and ordered a round of drinks on him. "I think we need to celebrate."

Sam was relieved. He hadn't been sure if A.J. would kill him or congratulate him and naturally the latter was preferable because Sarah had already done a great job of almost killing him several times. That was enough for him.

Updating Terri and A.J. took some time, and a lot of laughs, especially over the story of Sarah kicking Sam. Although the laughs were at Sam's expense he didn't mind because it actually got funnier the more it was told.

As the evening came to an end, Terri hugged Sam and both girls goodbye. A.J. followed suit but when he went to shake Sam's hand he pulled him aside to offer a bit of brotherly advice.

"I'm only going to say this once, Sam, if you hurt her, friends or not, you'll have me to deal with. She's been through enough and doesn't need to be hurt again."

CHAPTER TWENTY-FIVE

"You don't have to worry, A.J., Sarah is safe with me, but what you do have to remember is that I'm not necessarily safe with her." The two men laughed and said their goodnights.

"Well ladies, I must also say goodnight. Chloe, it was nice to meet you. I'm sure we will see each other again before you head back home. I work the next four nights so enjoy your time together and Sarah, I'll be talking to you tomorrow. Let me walk you to your car."

Standing in the parking lot, Chloe said good-bye to Sam and got into Sarah's car allowing them a little privacy to say goodnight. Sam took Sarah aside, put his arms around her and kissed her.

"Good night, Sarah. I love you. I'll miss you this weekend but admittedly it will give me a chance to recover."

Chuckling, Sarah offered, "I'm sorry again, Sam." Giving him another kiss she hopped into the car and headed home.

"Oh girl…he's one good-looking guy and you're in big trouble." Chloe teased.

TWENTY-SIX

THROUGHOUT THE REMAINDER OF THE week, the girls spent their time catching up with each other; going for walks, sitting in front of the fireplace, drinking wine and laughing until they cried. By Saturday night they decided it was time to hit the drive-in.

"You have one of those around here? Wow! I haven't been to a drive-in since I was a kid. Isn't it a little late in the year for that though? I mean it's the first week of November, Sarah." Chloe was slightly confused, figuring most drive-ins would wrap up by mid-October due to the cool weather.

"Not this place. Apparently, they stay open until mid-November. So let's grab some drinks and snacks and head over there. They start much earlier this time of year because it gets dark so early."

Packing up, the girls headed over to the Oak Leaf Drive-in. Finding a parking spot they were amazed at how many people actually attended regardless of the cool weather. Sarah glanced around and saw most everyone wearing coats with blankets over their legs. She figured that without heat and not being able to run engines, it likely got cold pretty quick.

"Chloe, let's go get some popcorn before the movie starts." Standing in line, Sarah felt a tap on her shoulder.

"Hi, Sarah." Turning around she was surprised to see Geoff standing there.

"Geoff! What a surprise to see you here." Sarah was noticeably uncomfortable and got the impression Geoff seemed pleased by that.

"Who's your beautiful friend?" Stepping forward Geoff reached his hand out to Chloe who was almost speechless. "Hi, I'm Geoff. A friend of...Sarah's."

"Um, hi, I'm Chloe. Also a friend of Sarah's."

Sarah was surprised to see Chloe immediately enamoured with Geoff. *She usually doesn't get this way. Chloe has always been the level-headed one*, she thought.

"Pleasure to meet you, Chloe. Are you just visiting?"

"Well, for another week or so, yes."

Oh my God, is Chloe actually blushing? Sarah's mouth dropped open. *Since when? This is completely unlike her.*

"Well, if Sarah wouldn't mind too much, I would love to steal you away one day and show you around the area."

Raising her eyebrows Sarah thought, *What?!*

"I would love that and I know Sarah wouldn't mind at all, would you, Sarah." Chloe couldn't take her eyes off of Geoff.

"No...I suppose not. Um, Chloe, we should get popcorn..." Sarah tried to interject.

"That's great! What are you doing on Monday, Chloe?"

Really? So soon? This guy is unbelievable.

CHAPTER TWENTY-SIX

"We don't want to miss the start of the movie..." Sarah again tried unsuccessfully to get her friend's attention.

"That would be great." Chloe was obviously smitten.

"But Chloe, Monday we were going to go into Westridge shopping..." Realizing she wasn't being heard at all she added, "Or…we don't have to." *Why am I bothering to even speak. They don't hear a word I'm saying.*

"Great! I'll pick you up at Sarah's by ten." Geoff seemed equally as smitten with Chloe.

"I'm looking forward to it." she smiled.

Giggling? Really? She's practically swooning! Sarah was amazed at the direction the conversation went and how quickly it went there.

"Until then pretty lady." Geoff flirted then bent over and kissed the top of Chloe's hand.

What the hell? Who does that anymore? Sarah didn't think she was jealous but she sure wasn't impressed.

"Looking forward to it Geoff. It was great to meet you…" Chloe stopped mid-sentence, smiled and waved with only her fingers as she watched Geoff leave.

Really? She practically batted her eyes at him. What the heck was that?

"So, Chloe. That's Geoff. I gather you liked him." Sarah had to contain her sarcasm.

"What? Oh…yes…I did…really like him, Sarah. My God he's a looker! You never told me about him." Chloe couldn't take her eyes off Geoff as he walked away.

Oh good, she finally took a breath.

"I was going to, but it just hadn't come up yet." Sarah wasn't sure how to respond to that but thought she managed pretty well, all things considered. *What was she supposed to say? Of course I didn't tell you about him because he was supposed to be devastated that I was no longer interested in him.*

"Wow, Chloe, I've never seen you so taken by a guy before."

"Well can you blame me? You saw him. He's so handsome! Maybe one night the four of us could all go out together? What do you think?"

"Oh, I don't think that's such a great idea right now, Chloe."

"Why not?"

Because the two men would kill each other over what just occurred less than a week ago, she wanted to say.

"Well, I suppose we could but why don't you go out with Geoff first and see what you think. Maybe you won't like him. First impressions are always a bit 'iffy'. You never really get to know someone that way."

"Ok but I'm sure I'll like him, Sarah. If I was to judge by first impressions, this man is hot! He kissed my hand! Who does that? Oh my God!" Chloe was still staring into space.

"Chloe." Sarah tried bringing her friend back down to earth.

"So, Sarah, are we going to get some popcorn or what? If we don't hurry up we'll miss the movie."

Sarah's mouth dropped open. *Really?*

Arriving home after the movie, Sarah unlocked the house door and hung up her coat, dropping the blankets on the bench by the door. "That was so much fun, Chloe. I was freezing by the end of the movie but it was nice to go just the same."

CHAPTER TWENTY-SIX

"I loved it! The only thing that could have made it more fun was if we had filled a thermos with hot toddies." Laughing Chloe hung up her coat and sat down at the kitchen table.

"You want something warm to drink? I'm freezing. How about a tea?" Sarah put the kettle on and pulled out the teapot.

"So, do you know Geoff very well, Sarah? What's he like? Tell me about him." Chloe was curious and wanted to hear more.

"What's to tell, Chloe? He's a great guy who Sam has known since high school. He's a firefighter…"

"A firefighter? Are you kidding me? Talk about the icing on the cake! Go on." Chloe's face had lit up like a light bulb and she grew increasingly excited the more she learned about Geoff.

Sarah updated Chloe on Geoff's past, carefully avoiding any mention that they had been on a date together and she could see Chloe's face soften with sympathy at hearing about his childhood.

Their evening was spent sipping on tea and talking about Geoff. Sarah was getting a little irritated with the conversation and decided to change the subject. She was still miffed by it all but was happy for her friend just the same.

"About tomorrow, Chloe. I was wondering if you would help me with float recruiting for our Christmas Eve parade. I promised Sam I would help him with it and I really haven't done much at this point. Would you mind if we went to a few places that are actually open tomorrow morning and then we can meet Terri for lunch."

"That sounds like fun, Sarah. I would love to help you out."

Sarah was thrilled to have her friend helping her and even more thrilled to have her visiting.

"Chloe, I really miss you. I wish you lived closer. If you ever get sick of that job of yours you could move here and then we could see each other all the time."

Sarah noticed that Chloe made no comment and seemed rather uncomfortable when she was talking about her job and decided not to push her.

As Sarah poured the tea, Chloe asked, "By the way, you know what I want for dinner while I'm here? Spaghetti. I've been craving it, what do you say?"

"You got it, Chloe. Spaghetti dinner Tuesday night it is. In the meantime would you like some cheese and crackers?" The girls spent the rest of the evening talking and laughing like old times.

TWENTY-SEVEN

GEOFF SHOWED UP AT EXACTLY ten o'clock Monday morning. Chloe had been ready by nine but would never have let on to Geoff how excited she was to see him again.

"Bye, Sarah, I'll see you later on," Chloe shouted as she ran out to meet Geoff in the driveway.

Before Sarah could even say anything, Chloe was gone, leaving Sarah to figure out how to fill the remainder of her day.

Calling her sister, Sarah was hopeful she was free. "Terri, just wondered if you wanted to go for lunch?"

"Barney's Burger Bar sounds perfect. See you soon."

Two hours later she found herself in a rather old, run-down establishment wondering if the food would be any better.

"So, this is Barney's Burger Bar?" Sarah wasn't exactly impressed but Terri had assured her that it was good food, so she was willing to trust her sister's recommendation. It was clean but not exactly high fashion as far as the decor was concerned. The walls were lined with mirrors; there were booths along the far wall and a few tables bolted to the floor in the middle of the room with seats attached. Everything seemed to be some shade of grey except for the walls that seemed to be pale yellow and in need of a fresh coat of paint. The floor was gray vinyl tile and along the opposite wall of the booths was an enclosed glass and stainless steel counter that had every condiment you could ever desire for your burger. It was a cash-only establishment, which was unusual these days and after ordering and paying for their food Terri and Sarah grabbed a booth and sat down until their food was ready.

"Where's Chloe? I'm surprised she didn't come with you?"

"You'll never believe this but she has gone out with Geoff." Sarah was a little embarrassed to even be admitting it. "I know it was only one date but he sure got over me rather fast didn't he?" she mused. "Don't get me wrong, I'm not interested in him, I suppose I'm just licking my bruised ego."

"I wouldn't worry about Geoff getting over you so quickly. That's Geoff, always has been. He has never really settled down with anyone for very long and truth be told he would have eventually moved on anyway."

"Well, thanks a lot!" Sarah laughed.

"It's nothing against you. It's just, Geoff! He can't settle with any one woman. It's not that he isn't sincere; it's just that he's a bit of a free spirit. Either that or he just gets cold feet. Didn't you say Chloe has been alone for a couple of years now? This will be good for her to get back in the game and not get hurt. The fact that she leaves in a week or so will work out well. Let her have her fun, Sarah." Terri was trying to be the voice of reason.

"Yeah, well, I don't like it at all. I don't want to see her get hurt and Geoff seems to fall in and out of 'like' rather quickly doesn't he," Sarah deliberated.

"Ladies, your food is up. What would you like on your burgers?"

CHAPTER TWENTY-SEVEN

"Thanks, Tom!" Terri called over.

Sarah was surprised. "Tom? I don't understand. Tom is the owner of Barney's you say?" Sarah laughed at the thought.

"That's right. There is no Barney, only a Tom." Terri giggled at her sister's perplexity and grabbing her food went to sit down and dig in.

There was just something about a juicy cheeseburger. It was comfort food. Sarah was enjoying every last bite of it and her onion rings too.

"How can you eat your onion rings with vinegar on them? I just can't even imagine." Terri scrunched up her nose at the thought.

"Yeah, but you hate vinegar. I love them that way and with lots of salt too." Popping an onion ring into her mouth Sarah added, "These milk shakes are the best I've ever had. I can see why you like coming here." Sarah finished the last of her burger and wiped her mouth.

"Well, Tom's a long time client of mine. He has bought and sold more than a dozen homes over the years. He loves to buy them; have them fixed up and then sell them again, always with a profit." Terri spoke quietly because she didn't want Tom overhearing her discussing his personal business.

"He keeps getting richer and so do I!" Terri chuckled. "I try to do as much business as possible with my clients outside of real estate. Keeps me in touch with them and in good standing and besides these really are the best burgers around."

Finishing their lunch, the girls bid Tom farewell and headed back to town.

Arriving at Terri and A.J.'s, Sarah thanked her sister for lunch, declining to go in for a visit. She really wanted to stop by Sam's and see what he was up to.

"Sam has been working nights these last four nights and I haven't seen him since Wednesday," she mused.

Sarah felt a little ill at ease talking so casually about her relationship with Sam. It was so new that it still felt a little awkward. Sarah loved the thought of having Sam in her life though. He excited her. When he called, her heart skipped a beat just hearing his voice. When his hand touched hers it was as if all else stopped and she was entirely focussed on that touch. She felt a bit like a giddy schoolgirl but she didn't care because she was happy for the first time in years.

Her time with Travis hadn't been easy. He was short-tempered and they had many an argument in the time they were together. Sadly, when she had met him, he was the quarterback that she fell hard for. He was handsome, tall, and larger than life. He was the star of the show and she fell madly in love with him, or so she thought. But as time went by, he began criticizing her. "Why are you wearing that dress?" or "Since when do you go out with your hair looking like that?" Little idiosyncrasies about her that seemed to get on his nerves the longer they stayed together.

Sarah hadn't realized until she had been apart from him that she had started losing her sense of 'self' being with him. She was becoming insecure; losing her confidence and her self-esteem. She just wanted to please him, keep him happy. She almost left once before after a party being held for his football team when they won the semi-finals. Travis had become quite drunk and started making snide comments about her in front of his teammates. She could tell everyone was uncomfortable with it and Sarah was so humiliated she left the party and walked home. It was late at night and she cried all the way home, which took over an hour to walk. Once there, she started to pack up her things to leave but before she could, Travis showed up. Realizing what was taking place he convinced her to stay. He said he would change, which he did…for a while at least, until she found him cheating on her. That was the end for her.

CHAPTER TWENTY-SEVEN

"Sarah? Where are you girl?"

Suddenly realizing Terri was talking to her and that she had been daydreaming, Sarah said, "I'm sorry Terri, what did you say?"

"I said, things seem to be going really well with you and Sam but just be sure you aren't jumping into something you may regret later on. It seems rather sudden if you ask me. Sam's a great guy but I'm worried that you're rebounding. Just keep yourself strong and don't fall into the same trap you did with Travis." Terri didn't want to see her little sister heartbroken again, although she knew Sam very well and knew how loyal and protective he was of those he loved.

"Don't worry, Terri. I feel that my heart is safe with Sam. There's just something about him that makes me feel so comfortable, like we're meant to be together. It all just seems to fit." Sarah's eyes sparkled and she couldn't help but smile. "Didn't you feel that way with A.J. when you met?"

Thinking back Terri smiled. "We were so young then, Sarah, but I suppose I did. A.J. was always the cocky, smug kid who dared anyone to challenge him and of course no one did. They knew by his size alone that no one was a match for him, and well, A.J. knew it too." Terri laughed. "Admittedly, I always did feel loved when I was with him and I knew my heart was safe too, so I guess I can understand how you're feeling."

Terri chuckled at her sister and gave her a hug. "Okay well, I'll trust your judgement, Lil' Sis. Now go see your man and I'll talk to you later on."

Sarah got into her own car and called Sam on her mobile phone before heading to his place.

"Hi, Sam. Where are you?"

"I'm in town at Old Bill's station. Where are you?"

"I'll be right there. Feel like going for a coffee?"

"Sounds great. We can go to Milroy's Deli beside Bill's. In fact, why don't I just meet you there."

Walking into Milroy's, Sarah was pleasantly surprised. The deli was very quaint and homey. There were even red and white checker tablecloths. *Real cloth. Unheard of these days.* There was a lunch counter with stools, all in red vinyl; a large menu board behind the counter high up on the wall where everyone could see it. There were booths aligning the windows and even an old jukebox in the far corner. The walls were lined with pictures dating back to the early 1900's when the restaurant was brand new and run by, not surprisingly, the Milroy family. Sarah didn't take the time to read the story behind each picture but she got the gist of it. She was impressed that although Hurricane Hazel had virtually destroyed the restaurant back in the 1950's, the Milroy's persevered, rebuilt and opened once again more than a year later to the elation of the town's Mayor at that time.

Looking at the pictures, Sarah hadn't seen Sam sneak up behind her and was pleasantly surprised when he put his arms around her waist and kissed her on the neck.

"Hey there, pretty lady. Whatcha doin'?"

Sarah closed her eyes and smiled, enjoying the intimacy and the overall sense of feeling loved. Wrapping her arms around Sam's, she leaned her head back into his chest and savoured the moment that quickly ended when the waitress called out, "Hey, Sam. How're doin'? Long time no see."

CHAPTER TWENTY-SEVEN

Unwrapping his arms from around Sarah, Sam smiled. "Well, Jules, my dear, I'm doing great. How are you doing? I've missed your smiling face," which was ironic since she wasn't smiling at all.

"I hear you kicked my sister out."

Sarah noted the sarcasm dripping with each word Jules uttered and was a little concerned about the direction the conversation was going.

"Yeah Jules, I kicked your sister out." Sam walked over to Jules and took a stance directly in front of her as he spoke.

The silence was deafening. Sarah felt uncomfortable and wasn't sure what to do, sit, stand or crawl under the nearest table to take cover. Suddenly laughter rang through the restaurant; Jules and Sam hugged leaving Sarah completely confused.

Laughing, Jules offered, "Good for you, Sam! She needed her ass kicked. That girl doesn't know a good man when she sees one and if she did, her collection of spiky God-awful shoes would take precedence over any man. Welcome back from hell, Sammy." Looking in Sarah's direction Jules asked, "So, who might you be, my dear?"

Sarah looked at the pair as if they had lost their minds.

"Hi, I'm Sarah. I'm pleased to meet you albeit a tad confused by that whole conversation. You mean you're Trish's sister?"

"I sure am. She's my younger sister who always spends more time holding her hand out to people than actually working for what she gets. She didn't recognize a good thing when she was with Sam and he was wise enough to kick her to the curb."

Sarah felt relief and sat down on one of the lunch counter stools.

Pouring Sam a coffee, Jules asked Sarah, "What can I get for you, Honey? Coffee?"

"I would love a tea if you don't mind, Jules."

After chatting with Jules for a few minutes, Sam and Sarah took their drinks to a booth to sit down and get a bit of privacy.

"So, where's Chloe? I thought she would be with you."

Sitting opposite each other Sarah explained the situation with Chloe and Geoff.

Just then Jules came by and filled up Sam's coffee mug. "Do you two lovebirds want any food or are you just surviving on liquids today?" Pulling some creamers out of her apron pocket, Jules placed them on the table in front of Sam.

"Not today, Jules."

"Alright. Too bad though, pot roast is on the menu." Jules walked back behind the counter once again and busied herself with making more coffee and going through the process of placing clean cutlery into the cutlery bin ensuring knives, forks and spoons were put into their proper places and carefully drying them if they were still wet.

Watching Jules work away Sarah was curious, "Okay, so first of all why is Jules wearing a nametag with the name Gillian on it?"

"That's because her actual name is Gillian but everyone just calls her Jules." Sam offered.

"I see. Okay so tell me how could Jules and Trish be sisters? I just don't see the connection in either looks or personality. Trish is all about herself and just plain rude with poufy red hair, loads of make-up, spikey heels and skinny jeans. Whereas, Jules is a sweetheart with short straight blonde hair, next to no make-up, comfortable shoes and a normal pair of jeans that I'm sure she doesn't have to peel off at the end of the day. They are polar opposites." Sarah chuckled at the thought of Trish possibly lying on her bed at night struggling to get those tight jeans off.

CHAPTER TWENTY-SEVEN

"Oh they are. I had met Jules first and thought if her sister were anything like her I would hit the jackpot. Well needless to say, I was wrong." Laughing almost to himself, Sam was reflective. "As much as I hate to admit it, I think I was more interested in Trish for her looks."

Sarah's mouth dropped open in disbelief and sarcastically added, "Really? You don't say."

Hearing her tone, Sam quickly looked up and seeing her disbelief realized how ridiculous his comment must have sounded. "Aw c'mon, give me a break. That's a bit of a double standard don't you think? You told me that you initially dated this Travis guy because of his looks."

"Admittedly, I was taken by the fact that he was a football player and I thought he was rugged and cute. Okay, okay so I suppose it is a bit of a double standard." Laughing together they walked to the cash to pay their bill.

"The coffee's on me, Sam. I figure it's the least I can do considering how my sister treated you."

"That's not necessary Jules. Now, what do I owe you?"

"I told you, Honey, this one's on me. Now get outta' here before I change my mind. It was nice to meet you, Sarah. You've got a good one here, don't let him go." Jules smiled and headed over to a table at the far end of the diner, giving a wave back to them before taking the new order.

Sam threw two dollars on the counter as a tip and opened the door for Sarah to leave.

"Sarah, I have some hay deliveries to make. Did you want to come along for the ride and I'll treat you to dinner at the pub?"

"Sure, Sam. Sounds like fun, although I have no right going out for dinner as well. I had a huge lunch with Terri today at Barney's Burgers. Ever heard of the place?"

"Sure, Barney's Burgers has been around since I was a kid. A little off the beaten path but the food there is awesome, especially those onion rings."

"You can say that again," Sarah laughed.

"Well don't worry, you'll be working all that food off unloading hay bales with me," Sam laughed. "So let's go."

Having made all of the hay deliveries Sarah and Sam headed to the Old Beagle by six o'clock where they found an empty booth in a far corner of the pub.

Just as they finished dinner Sarah looked up to see Geoff and Chloe walk in the door looking for a table to sit at. Sarah waved them over and they all moved to a bigger table.

Noticing Geoff and Chloe snuggling in closer to each other, Sarah was beginning to feel uncomfortable and tried to brush it off with conversation.

"So, how has your day been?" Sarah tried not to sound too acrimonious as she asked. She didn't want Geoff thinking she actually cared how quickly he'd moved on from her.

It was Chloe who answered. "We had such a nice day, Sarah. Geoff took me to a beautiful hiking spot called Wallace Point that overlooks Forestville. The view is spectacular. Have you heard of it?"

Not even moving her head, Sarah's eyes looked dryly in Geoff's direction. Quickly grabbing his beer Geoff started gulping it down avoiding Sarah's gaze. Looking back at Chloe, Sarah answered, "Why, yes, as a matter of fact I have heard of it Chloe."

CHAPTER TWENTY-SEVEN

"It's so beautiful. We hiked awhile and then Geoff surprised me with a picnic in this beautiful open area in the middle of the woods. It included champagne and a campfire. Wasn't that romantic?" Chloe was captivated.

Sarah just kept staring Geoff down and without taking her eyes off of him deprecatingly added, "Oh, it's romantic alright, Chloe."

Geoff cleared his throat and asked, "Does anyone want another beer? It's hot in here."

Sam started to laugh out loud, helping to relax the moment. He could see the man squirming under Sarah's judging eyes but decided he deserved what he was getting.

Seeing the look on Sarah's face and how she was staring at Geoff and knowing her as well as she did, Chloe could tell something was up and it didn't take long for her to understand.

"No way! Are you kidding me?" Chloe pulled away from Geoff so she could look him in the face. "You didn't…did you?" she asked with an air of irritation. "Did you actually take other girls there as well?"

Sarah just about spit out her drink and Geoff glared at her. Sarah caught herself so as not to exacerbate the situation. *This is karma my friend and it looks good on you.*

"Well…" Geoff avoided looking at Sarah while struggling to find the right words. As usual Chloe didn't miss a trick.

"No! You didn't! Sarah too? Geoff you're unbelievable!" Chloe wasn't really angry, just somewhat annoyed that this hadn't been unique to her and Geoff.

"That's pathetic. You could've been a little more original. Honestly, that's just not right!" Chloe was feigning hurt and shaking her head while Sarah and Sam roared with laughter at Geoff's expense.

"Yeah, yeah enough already you guys." Geoff wasn't feeling at all comfortable and it didn't help that Sam and Sarah took pleasure in watching him squirm.

Sarah felt it was just about time to let Geoff off the hook.

"Listen Chloe, when Geoff and I went there he certainly didn't have a picnic lunch with champagne…" Sarah lied more for the benefit of her friend than for Geoff's comfort. "…so you can be sure it was special and I'm sure quite romantic." Sarah looked over at Geoff who realized he was being given a reprieve and gave her an uncomfortable smile and a nod.

Thankfully everything was more amicable than Sarah had originally feared with the remainder of the evening being enjoyed by all.

TWENTY-EIGHT

Over the next several days Sarah didn't see much of Chloe who always seemed to be out with Geoff. Sarah had wanted to spend more time with her friend before she had to leave and was feeling a little resentful that she wasn't getting the quality time with Chloe that she had anticipated.

Waking up Thursday morning, Sarah discovered that Chloe had left the house early and assumed that she had, yet again, met up with Geoff. Still not sure how she felt about Chloe and Geoff together, Sarah had to admit though that she hadn't seen her friend this happy in a very long time.

Hearing her cell phone ring Sarah ran in her pajamas to answer it. Seeing that it was Travis, she decided to pick it up and then quickly hang it up again. She didn't even want him leaving a message. *What the hell is wrong with him? He seems to be getting worse. The Travis I knew would never have been so heartless.* Her palms were sweaty and she was nervous at the thought of having to deal with Travis and now wished she had spoken to Sam or A.J. about him.

Just then the phone rang again. Sarah panicked, afraid it was Travis but daring to look, she smiled with relief and picked it up.

"Daddy! How are you doing? I miss you and Mom so much. How are you feeling? When are you coming to visit me again? Guess who's here visiting now?"

"Kiddo! One question at a time, please. First of all, I'm doing fine. I had my last check-up with the doctor yesterday, stitches out and got a clean bill of health."

"What's that, Karen? Okay, well almost a clean bill of health. I can't do any heavy lifting for a few months, or so he says."

"What, Karen? Yes, I told her. No I haven't told her that because you keep talking to me, I haven't had a chance to."

"So, your mother and I want to come out again to help you finish things up, assuming of course that you still have things to do. We were going to come out the end of November sometime and stay for a couple of weeks. How does that sound?"

"Karen, I'll ask her in a minute. No, I won't ask her that. It's none of your business anyway."

"Daddy?"

"No, Karen I won't, the girl deserves her privacy"

"Daddy?" Sarah was shaking her head listening to her father converse with her mother and wondering why her mother just didn't call herself.

"What's that, Kiddo?"

"Daddy, tell Mom I'll talk to her in a minute." Sarah was starting to get a little annoyed with the three-way conversation.

"Karen! Sarah will talk to you in a minute. Stop interrupting me." George was irritated.

CHAPTER TWENTY-EIGHT

"Like I say, Sarah, the doctor says I can't do any heavy lifting, which I personally think is a bunch of bullshit. I'm as healthy as a horse. He doesn't know what the hell he's talking about but I can do most everything else."

"And yes, Daddy, you and Mom can come anytime you want. Chloe is here but she will be leaving long before then."

"Okay Sarah, I'm going to put your mother on but God help you because she is going to pry into your personal life, so be prepared."

With that Sarah could hear her father telling her mother in the background not to intrude, that it was none of her business, but if she insisted on doing this then here's the damn phone. Sarah laughed to herself listening to the commentary.

"Sarah dear? It's Mom." Sarah smiled. As if she couldn't have figured that out without being told.

"Hi, Mom. How are you doing? I miss you and Daddy so much." Sarah was excited to speak with her mother although she knew exactly where the conversation was going to lead.

"Sarah, are you dating that nice young man, Sam? You never tell us anything dear and I think it's only fair that you let us know. We need to know you are taken care of dear."

"Mother, I don't need taking care of. I'm a very capable, independent woman who doesn't need any man to take care of her. Now, to answer your question, as a matter of fact I am dating Sam. He's a really great guy." Sarah was happy to share this information with her mother and it seemed her mother was as well.

"Oh that's wonderful, dear. I'm so glad to hear this. Now listen, have you slept with him yet because..."

"Mother! That's a very personal question!" Sarah couldn't believe her mother would pry like this.

"No George, I think it is very relevant to ask."

"Now listen, be sure to use protection, dear. You don't want to be getting pregn…"

"Mother! Please stop!" Sarah was mortified.

"But George…" Sarah could hear her mother respond to her father's obviously adamant interjection.

"I realize that Geor…yes of course, you are right." Refocusing her conversation with Sarah, Karen spoke very quietly and added, "Now Sarah dear, you know you can come to me anytime about anything…"

"Mother, you gave me the birds and bees lecture a long time ago and seriously, I'm a big girl and I don't need you offering me advice about my sex life, thank you very much. It's disgusting! Honestly! Daddy's right, it's none of your business!" Sarah was shaking her head in disbelief at the direction of the conversation and was ready to hang up.

Speaking normally again Karen said, "Yes, we will be coming to help you out around the house and…what? Oh...okay fine, George… your father wants to speak to you again."

Sarah could hear a bit of a kerfuffle on the other end of the phone line "…stop it, Karen…" and "…meant well…I'm her mother…" and "… give me the phone" and with that George came on the line once again.

"Sarah, ignore your mother. She obviously doesn't know when to butt the hell out of your life."

"Okay, so Sarah, now that your mother has left the room I just want to say I'm happy for you, Kiddo, but you make sure that young man knows that if he hurts you he'll wish he never lived or breathed near you.

Am I making myself perfectly clear? Now, that's all I have to say about that and whatever you do don't tell your mother I said anything or I'll never hear the end of it."

Laughing at the entire conversation she had been having with her parents, Sarah assured her father that she would be fine. "Sam isn't Travis. He's a great guy and besides I think if he hurt me you would have to get in line behind me and then A.J. to deal with him."

Sarah was growing tired of this conversation and decided it was time to wrap it up.

"I have to go now, Daddy, and head into town to find Chloe. She's leaving soon and I promised her we would go shopping today…although I think she forgot. I'll see you and Mom in a few weeks. Okay?" Sarah just wanted to get off the phone.

Hanging up from the incredibly uncomfortable conversation with her mother and smiling at how protective her father was, Sarah jumped in the shower. Still not having heard from Chloe, Sarah decided she would head into town to see if she could find her and if not, track down Sam.

The hot water felt good on this chilly November day and Sarah savoured the long steamy shower she was having and her moment of peace. Standing under the water stream Sarah enjoyed the feel of the water trickling through her hair and gliding slowly down her body. It was almost hypnotizing. Clearing her mind, she stood there completely enveloped by the satiny blanket of water. Within moments she was pleasantly surprised by the feel of someone's strong hands slowly making their way around her waist from behind. Knowingly, Sarah smiled as she felt Sam's body slip into the shower and embrace her from behind. Letting out a contented sigh at the feel of his body against hers she felt him kiss the back of her neck as his hands slowly found their way to her breasts where they massaged soap around her nipples, gently arousing her whole body. Continuing to use his right hand to slowly knead her nipples with his fingers, Sam used his left hand to work its way between her legs, gently stroking until she couldn't take it anymore. Moaning out loud Sarah grabbed Sam's hand and enjoyed the combined movement of bringing her nearly to climax. Turning Sarah to face him, Sam picked her up, then slowly lowered her down and gently slid into her. Sarah was, at this moment, feeling grateful for her over-sized shower. Leaning forward, wrapping her arms around his neck, Sam suckled on Sarah's nipples and they moved in unison until, moaning out loud, they shuddered together in ecstasy. Enjoying the moment, they held their position until Sam slowly eased Sarah to standing, kissing her gently but passionately on the lips.

"I was looking for the right moment to come see you and I'm guessing you would agree the timing was perfect," Sam whispered.

"Oh I'd say so." Sarah felt like she was in a bit of a stupor. This was a moment of pure bliss and she was taking it all in. She didn't want it to end. This man knew how to keep her wanting more.

Getting out of the shower still dripping wet, they headed to her bedroom where Sarah laid down on the bed and Sam began kissing her gently. Starting with her lips he slowly worked his way along her neck and chest, then to her breasts where his tongue worked its magic on her nipples until Sarah could barely breath. From there he worked his way down to her stomach where he seemed to kiss every inch of her wet bare skin until finally his tongue found its way between her legs where it slowly but expertly sent her body into climactic convulsions.

"Oh my God, Sam, I love you!" Sarah whispered, barely getting out the words.

Then before she realized it, Sam slid into her and within moments felt his body shudder in response to the motion of their two bodies bringing them both to a place neither had been with anyone in a very long time.

TWENTY-NINE

"THANKS FOR PICKING ME UP and dropping me off, Terri. I didn't want to wake Sarah when I left. It's been an exciting morning and I appreciate all your support." Chloe opened the passenger door of Terri's car. "Did you want to come in?"

Seeing that Sam's truck was in the driveway and knowing Sarah would wonder why she and Chloe were out together, Terri opted to head into the office instead. "No thanks, but listen, Chloe, I think you are making the right decision and I can certainly help you with the transition. I won't say anything to Sarah. That's up to you. I'll get back to you as soon as I hear, which should be within the next day or two and with any luck everything can be wrapped up before you leave next week. I don't anticipate any problems." Terri waved good-bye to Chloe as she backed out of the driveway and headed to the office.

"Oh my God, Sam. Was that a car door I heard?" Sarah scrambled to throw the blankets off so she could get dressed, pushing Sam with her feet out of her bed and onto the floor.

"What the hell!" Sam had fallen asleep and awoke to find himself falling onto the floor.

"Sam, get dressed. I think Chloe's home." Sarah was frantically putting on her jeans and bra. *Oh my God. Can a girl not make out with her boyfriend without even one person walking in on her? This is becoming a bad habit.*

"Sarah, where are you?"

"I'm in my room changing, Chloe. I'll be right out." Sarah tossed Sam's clothes at him and mouthed the words 'get dressed now'. Yelling out to Chloe, Sarah asked, "So where were you this morning Chloe? Out with Geoff?"

"Is Sam here, Sarah? I see his truck."

"Um…no. I mean…yes, Sam's here. He's in my ensuite fixing the toilet. It was…um…backed up." *Really Sarah? Your toilet is backed up? Couldn't you have come up with something a bit more convincing?*

Sam mouthed the words, 'Really? The toilet?' to which she shrugged her shoulders and then gave him a non-verbal signal to get a move on. He whispered that he was dressing as fast as he could.

Finally dressed, Sarah fussed with her hair, which was a mess because it had dried haphazardly when she fell asleep. Knowing there was no hope for making it look presentable, she walked out to see Chloe in the kitchen, who looked at Sarah knowingly and smiled.

"Really? A backed-up toilet, Sarah? You could have done better than that." Chloe chuckled.

Sighing, Sarah called, "Come out, Sam, she knows." And with that Sam walked out of Sarah's bedroom smiling, his hair tussled and shirt half-buttoned and off kilter.

CHAPTER TWENTY-NINE

"Hey, Chloe, how's it going?"

"Great, Sam. How are you; or do I need to even ask?" Chloe looked dryly at Sarah who rolled her eyes and looked away.

"Where'd you go this morning, Chloe? I didn't know you had a date with Geoff." Sarah started pulling things out to make coffee and sandwiches knowing that she was starving and expected Sam was as well.

"Well, that's what I need to talk to you about, Sarah. I haven't been completely honest with you."

Sarah stopped what she was doing and looked questioningly at Chloe. She suddenly felt a sense of concern.

"What's going on, Chloe? Is everything okay?" Sarah waited patiently for a response.

"Well, I should leave you ladies to talk." Sam offered.

"No, Sam, that's okay. It isn't that big of a deal really. You see, I lost my job a few weeks ago which is why I came out here to see you, Sarah."

Sarah's mouth dropped open in shock. "Chloe, I feel terrible...you've been there so long. Seven years or something like that right?"

"No wait, Sarah, hear me out. This story has a happy ending. I actually talked to Terri the other day, which is who I was out with this morning. I asked her to look around for a home for me and she found one. I'm happy to say that I'm hoping to be your neighbour in a couple of months."

Suddenly Sarah screamed, and running around the counter gave Chloe a bear hug lifting her off the ground. Jumping up and down in each other's arms the girls screamed with excitement as Sam just smiled and shook his head. Deciding to let the girls talk, Sam got coffee brewing and started making sandwiches.

"Chloe, I'm so happy about this. Well, not happy you lost your job but so happy you'll be living near me. Why didn't you tell me earlier? I could have helped you look for a place."

"Well, I hadn't really thought of it until Terri took me out on my own the first time but then after that Geoff and I went out looking together. He's been wonderful and helped me to make a decision. He really is a great guy, Sarah."

Yeah well, if you hurt her Geoff I'll bust your sorry ass. As much as Sarah hated to admit it her friend and Geoff did make a cute couple.

"Chloe, this is such wonderful news. So where did you buy? Where are you going to work?" Sarah was getting excited at the thought of Chloe living in the same town.

Chloe explained that it was a small place the other side of town in a new subdivision that had been built the previous year. Because it was empty, if her offer was accepted, she would be able to move in whenever she was ready.

"So, I decided I would move in right after the new year, which would give me time to go back home, pack up and arrange to get my stuff moved out here. I'm so excited, Sarah! A new beginning."

Sarah could completely identify with that thought and smiled, seeing her friend so delighted.

"Okay Ladies, enough chit chat. I've made coffee and sandwiches. I don't know about you but I'm starving, so let's eat." Sam placed the platter of sandwiches in the middle of the table and poured coffee for everyone.

Looking at him, Sarah grinned seeing his shirt buttoned off kilter. Realizing she had been completely ignoring him, she mouthed the words, 'Thank you,' to which he just grinned as he passed her a coffee.

CHAPTER TWENTY-NINE

"I haven't found a job just yet but with my severance package I have enough to get by for several months until I find one, but I'm sure something will come up once I move here. Terri even suggested getting my real estate license and working with her. So I have options to consider."

Sarah and Sam enjoyed listening to Chloe tell them all about the house. "I'm just waiting to hear back from Terri to see if my offer is accepted."

"Chloe, that's only ten minutes from my place! This is going to be awesome!" Things were just getting better and better as far as Sarah was concerned.

When Sam left mid-afternoon the girls decided to take advantage of the beautiful fall day and go for a walk before dark instead of going shopping. When they returned home, Sarah was surprised to see her side door slightly ajar and assumed they hadn't shut it tight until she noticed a black marker on the kitchen table. Her heart skipped a beat. Her phone rang and knowing it would likely be Travis, she ignored it. She didn't want to give him the satisfaction of scaring her.

"Aren't you going to answer that?" Chloe asked.

Momentarily distracted, Sarah responded, "No I'll let it go to voicemail, Chloe. Did you want to do something tonight?"

"Oh, that sounds great, Sarah, but I'm going out with Geoff tonight. I'm sorry. I know I've been neglecting you this week. How about we go tomorrow night. I'll reserve the entire day for you and I to go shopping and spend the evening together." Chloe was hopeful her friend wouldn't be too hurt.

"Sure, Chloe, that's fine. No worries." Sarah would have preferred not to stay home but understood why her friend wanted to see Geoff. He was a very charming man.

After Chloe left, Sarah looked over at her answering machine. Seeing the message light flashing she decided to listen to it. As expected, it was from Travis.

"How's Chloe doing, Sarah? Not that I give a fuck, I never really liked her, although I'm entirely sure the feeling was mutual. Does she like your new boyfriend? Was she as surprised as I was at how quickly you moved on?" There was a break in the message for a few seconds and then he continued.

"You know, Sarah, you should really learn to lock your doors. Anyone could break in. It just isn't safe. And by the way, you left something on the floor of the garage, Baby. I thought you might want it back. Oh, and Sarah, I'll be seeing you real soon, you can count on it."

She felt numb. The palms of her hands were sweaty and she was feeling jittery. He was stalking her and knew it was time to involve A.J., but hesitated while Chloe was visiting. What bothered her was that this had become more than just your average breakup. She kept hoping Travis would cool off and it would all stop. *I'll give it until Chloe leaves and if he bothers me again I'll get A.J. involved.*

THIRTY

During Chloe's final week visiting, Sarah was grateful to be able to spend quality time with her friend before she headed back home again. When the day came for Chloe to leave, Sarah waved good-bye but, instead of regretting that her friend was leaving, she was excited for her to come back again. She was also pleased that she hadn't heard from Travis again and was hopeful it would continue.

In some ways Sarah was grateful for some time alone. Things had been a little hectic since she moved to Forestville and she needed a break before her parents came out in a week or so. Remembering that she was supposed to finish helping Sam with the float recruiting, Sarah decided to venture out on her own that week. She had the time and wanted to get the job done. She knew how busy Sam had been at work with training and figured he would be happy not having to worry about it and besides, she wanted to do something productive for a change.

As the week progressed, Sarah managed to get a dozen businesses that agreed to put floats into the parade. The high school and service group marching bands also agreed, as well as some smaller groups around town who always either put a float or a group of people in, marching or handing out candy. The Christmas Eve parade was coming together nicely.

She even managed to get Joe from Joe's Hardware to put in a float. It didn't take much. Sarah just had to tell him he was the only business in town not putting one in and how would that look for business and Joe was convinced, not to mention the ten percent discount she offered him on his entry fee which sweetened the deal. Sam will be so pleased this job is done, she thought as she dialled up his number.

As expected, Sam was very happy and asked Sarah to meet him for dinner at the Old Beagle that night. She was looking forward to this because she hadn't seen much of Sam while Chloe was visiting and knew that once her parents arrived her time with him would be limited once again.

Placing their food order, Sam asked, "So, did Chloe hear back about that house offer she had in?"

"Yes she did and she got it, with a bit of negotiating. She'll be moving early in January."

"It's funny, Geoff seems to be quite taken with Chloe. I've never seen him so interested in someone before." Sam was amazed at this because Geoff never seemed to settle down with anyone in the past.

"In fact, from what I understand, they've been talking everyday since she left. He apparently plans on going out to help her pack up. He even offered to help her on moving day. Not at all like the Geoff I know."

"I know what you mean. I spoke to Chloe yesterday and she said the same thing, that Geoff has been calling everyday and was planning to visit her. I just hope they don't rush things, which I realize sounds hypocritical coming from me."

"Well, we need to leave them alone. They're adults and can sort it out for themselves, but I'll be shocked if it lasts. Geoff has commitment issues from a long way back."

CHAPTER THIRTY

"I've kept my mouth shut but I have to admit Chloe is happier than I've ever seen her and I really do hope it works out between them now. There's been a huge change in her since she met Geoff, a good change."

"Hey Sam, I keep meaning to ask you - have all of those puppies been adopted yet? I was considering adopting one of them. It would be nice to have one as company but also for security. You can't be too careful these days. A.J. always says that a dog is your best security."

Chuckling, Sarah tried not to show Sam that she had any concern about her safety but admittedly, Travis had made her uncomfortable. *I honestly don't think he would hurt me but he has certainly made me nervous enough that I'm thinking twice about being alone at the lake now.*

Sarah could see Sam looking at her inquisitively. She didn't want him asking too many questions and added, "It would help my mom and dad feel better about me being on my own at the lake…which is the reason I ask. You know parents…always worrying about nothing." Awkwardly laughing, Sarah was trying to be as nonchalant as possible. It must have worked because the look on Sam's face relaxed.

"I'm not sure if there are any pups left but I'll call Lisa at the shelter and ask for you."

The rest of dinner was spent catching up from the prior week and a discussion about Sarah's parents coming back to visit. Sam was pleased to hear her dad was doing so well and said he was looking forward to meeting him when he wasn't on a stretcher going to the hospital.

"My parents should be coming by the end of November for a couple of weeks, but beware of my mother. She's nosy and has no boundaries."

The evening flew by and before she knew it Sarah was saying good night to Sam before heading home.

"I would invite myself back to your place but I have to work in the morning and I have no intention of getting Spud mad by being late. He's been riding my case from day one and I don't need any reason for him to continue," Sam lamented.

Laughing, Sarah kissed Sam good-bye and wished him luck with Spud in the morning. Arriving at home, Sarah got out of her car and stopped cold. She had an overwhelming feeling that she was being watched yet scanning the dark yard as best she could she saw nothing unusual and shrugged it off, deciding it must have been the wind blowing through the trees that gave the eerie feel to the night, not to mention her overactive fear that Travis was stalking her. Shivering, Sarah headed into the house. *Boy, the temperature has dropped tonight. I may have to put the furnace on after all.* Thinking back to her evening with Sam and how much she enjoyed being around him, she smiled. Putting her pajamas on, Sarah crawled into bed and fell into a deep sleep.

As she slept Sarah heard the faint ringing of a phone. She was in such a deep sleep that she couldn't shake herself to fully wake up and happily fell back to sleep again. In the morning she awoke feeling rested and content.

Showering and getting dressed, Sarah smiled at the thought that she might be getting a dog. When she was growing up she had a golden retriever named Bubba. They had been inseparable and when the day came for Bubba to be put down Sarah cried inconsolably. There was nothing her parents could do or say to make her feel any better about not having her lifelong friend by her side anymore. She didn't care that Bubba was fourteen years old; she didn't care if he was too unhealthy to live a productive life; she didn't care about any of that. All she cared about was that she no longer had her best friend.

Tears came to her eyes as she reflected back on that horrible day but quickly shook herself out of it. *I'm going to get myself one of those adorable pups, that sweet blonde one I hope. It will be nice to have the company around here, not to mention feeling protected.*

CHAPTER THIRTY

♡ ♡ ♡

The next couple of weeks flew by and Sarah was excited at the prospect of her parents visiting. She was feeling particularly elated because she hadn't heard from Travis since before Chloe left and was hoping he had finally given up bothering her. Add that to the fact that she was especially excited for her parents to meet Sam (as her boyfriend this time). Just then Sarah heard a car door slam and she ran excitedly out to the driveway.

"Mom, Dad, it's so good to see you. Daddy, just leave those suitcases. I'll get them." Sarah didn't want her dad overdoing it.

"Now don't you start with that bullshit, Sarah. Your mother has been doing that to me since I got home from the hospital. I'm fine!" George scowled at the thought of the women in his family thinking he was helpless. *I'm not God damned helpless! I can carry a bloody suitcase for chrissakes.* George was annoyed already and they had just arrived.

"Sarah, if I'm going to be here I want no more of it. Give me some credit to know what I am and am not capable of doing and if I were you I would keep your mother in check as well." George looked in Karen's direction, raised his eyebrows and gave her a knowing nod. *There, that will keep Karen off my back for now. God damn that woman worries too much!*

Karen was about to say something when George gave her a look of, 'If you say one word Karen I'm gonna lose it,' then reconsidered.

Turning to Sarah she asked, "So Sarah dear, when are we going to meet Sam again?" and with that George and Sarah looked at each other and laughed. The rest of the day was rather uneventful and was spent catching up. Terri called later in the day and they accepted an invitation to have dinner with her and A.J. the next night.

Sunday was spent fixing all the little things around the house that just weren't right as far as George was concerned. He managed to get the washroom taps fixed so that hot was hot and cold was cold, replaced some lights and plugs in the house and by then it was time to freshen up and head to Terri's for dinner.

Greeting them at the door, A.J. gave Karen a big hug and shook George's hand as he welcomed them inside. Terri was just as excited to see her father and mother as Sarah had been. The dinner was spent catching up on George's health, Sarah's love life and, true to form, Karen couldn't resist asking Terri and A.J. when they were going to make her a grandmother.

"Good God, Karen. Why do you pry into these girls' lives like that?" George was annoyed, but laughed it off. He knew the girls could handle themselves but always felt compelled to try and head her off at the pass to help them out. Taking a drink of his beer, he just sat back and listened to the conversation. George enjoyed seeing his family together, laughing and enjoying each other's company. Chuckling to himself he was quite amused at the sight of A.J. rolling his eyes as Terri tried to keep her mother out of their 'baby' business. Then looking over at Sarah, he smiled watching her sit back with satisfaction knowing that her sister was in their mother's radar for a change. George loved the three ladies in his life and was fiercely protective. Once Terri married A.J., George knew he didn't have to worry about her anymore. A.J. was just as loving and protective as he was but Sarah…well, Sarah he worried about. His youngest daughter always was their biggest challenge. She was the spontaneous one; the one who went with her heart not her head.

It wasn't that they ever had to worry about Sarah sticking up for herself because she had no problem with that. *I'm sure there were several kids from school who learned that the hard way*, he chuckled at the thought. *Yes, Sarah certainly has a temper. I can't imagine what that Sam guy went through when he met her after the accident. God knows, she likely tore a strip off him.*

CHAPTER THIRTY

No, George mainly worried about Sarah when it came to matters of her heart. She didn't fall often, but when she fell, it was hard and when it came to Travis, George had been very concerned. She seemed to be blind to Travis and there had been no telling her otherwise. She was as stubborn as her father. George knew that if she fell for this Sam guy like she had Travis that his youngest daughter would get hurt again and George wasn't about to allow that to happen. *Which is exactly why I intend on speaking to A.J. later about this Sam character and find out exactly what kind of person he is. No son-of-a-bitch is going to hurt my daughter again. You can be sure of that.*

"Isn't that right, Daddy?" Terri asked.

"What was that, Hon?" George loved his oldest daughter. The day she was born he just stood staring down at her in his arms in complete disbelief that she was even his. She was beautiful and his sense of protectiveness set in the moment he set eyes on her. There was no going back. Being father to these two beautiful girls was what made his life complete. He loved his wife beyond words but his daughters were what kept him going through all the rough days.

He had to admit that when he first met A.J. he was sceptical. Big kid, a little too confident for George's liking especially when they first met. He had walked right up to George, shook his hand and said, "Hello Sir! I'm here to take your daughter Terri to the dance and you can be sure she's as safe with me, if not safer, as she would be with you."

What the hell? What twenty-one-year-old little shit says that to the father of the girl he is about to take out? Son-of-a-bitch should know that no one could protect my daughter like me, God dammit!

Although he was annoyed, George's response was more subdued than he really wanted it to be. Shaking A.J.'s hand, he didn't let it go but instead leaned in and whispered into his ear, "By God, Son, she had better be or you will wish you had never been born. Do we have an understanding?"

George laughed thinking back to that conversation. He remembered looking at A.J. as he stood there, watching the colour slowly leave his face. Then, unwaveringly, A.J. looked George straight in the eye and replied, "Don't you worry, Mr. Roberts. If anyone bothers Terri I'll punch the living shit right out of the little fuckers!" It was at that moment that George knew he liked A.J. Winston. *The kid had balls!*

"Daddy! What are you laughing at? This isn't funny! Oh my God, you aren't even listening!"

"What's that Terri? Of course I'm listening. You want me to pick sides between you and your mother and I'm sorry, Baby, but you know I can't do that. I have to go home with your mother. Now if it was between you and A.J., well you know I would pick you all the way." Laughing, George winked at A.J., who was smiling and shaking his head in disbelief.

The rest of the evening was spent playing cards, drinking and laughing until it was time to say goodnight. As the ladies hugged and said their good-byes, George took A.J. aside to have a talk with him.

"Now A.J., what's this Sam character like? He had better not hurt my little girl or he'll have me to deal with." George's tone was quite serious; A.J. knew this about his father-in-law. He was very protective of the ladies in his life and A.J. needed to reassure him that Sam was worthy of Sarah.

"Don't worry George. Sam is a 'no bull-shit' kind of guy. I've known him my whole life and I know he'll be good to Sarah. There's no problem there, I can assure you. But quite frankly if he did hurt her you would have to stand in line behind me to deal with him." A.J. didn't even crack the slightest smile. This was serious business to George and A.J. treated it that way.

Staring into A.J.'s eyes, George was trying to get a feel for the conversation and if he was being taken seriously. After a moment he relaxed, knowing he could trust what A.J. said about Sam.

CHAPTER THIRTY

"Okay, Son, I'm trusting you on this one." George gave A.J. a quick pat on the back. Putting his arm around his shoulders, George walked with him to the front door where the ladies were still talking. Shaking A.J.'s hand goodnight, George turned and gave Terry a hug and kiss then ushered Sarah and Karen out the front door.

Watching them leave, A.J. laughed at the conversation he had just had with his father-in-law knowing it needed to be taken seriously or George would have his ass. A.J. respected his father-in-law a great deal. They seemed to have gained an understanding early on and, albeit George intimidated A.J. when they first met, A.J. had been determined not to show it. His own father had walked out on their family when A.J. was in his early teens and over the years George became the father figure A.J. had longed for.

THIRTY-ONE

"Yes, Friday night. Are you free, Sam?"

"Sounds great, Sarah. I'm looking forward to meeting your mom and dad under more pleasant circumstances." Sam was more enthusiastic than Sarah thought he should be.

"Sam, I don't think you fully comprehend the situation here. My mom and dad won't go easy on you. My dad will be drilling you to make sure you aren't a serial killer or someone who is going to run off with his daughter and break her heart. My mom on the other hand will want assurances that you *will* run off with her daughter, make an honest woman out of her and drill you as to when and where you plan on proposing and giving her those grandbabies. You have no idea how invasive my parents can be." Sarah was concerned that her parents would scare off Sam for good. *God knows after Travis Dad is more intense than ever.*

"Listen, Sarah, I've dealt with worse parents than yours. Trust me they will be a piece of cake. Don't worry, everything will be fine." Sam was chuckling over what he felt were Sarah's unwarranted worries. "Really, it will be fine."

"I've also invited A.J. and Terri so you won't feel completely zeroed in on by my parents. Be warned though, regardless, they'll be giving you the third degree." Sarah was joking with Sam but had to admit she was a little worried about her parents with him. Especially her mother, who never kept her mouth shut and asked all the questions most people would only think to ask. There was not much of a filter on her mother.

Friday night arrived and Sarah couldn't relax. "Now Mom, Dad, don't be too intrusive with Sam. I don't want you imposing. It's not like we are running off and getting married or anything. We have just started dating and getting to know each other. I don't need you guys ruining this for me. He's a great guy but if you embarrass me I'll kill you both and hide your bodies." Sarah was clearly joking but a small part of her was completely serious.

"Honestly Sarah dear, you exaggerate. When have we ever imposed too mu..." her mother began then stopped when she saw the look of cynicism on her husband's face.

"Mother. I'm not kidding. You know very well what I mean." Sarah was getting frustrated. Her nerves were getting the best of her and she was in no mood for her mother's antics.

"Okay, fine, I'll try." her mother was having difficulty trying to sound convincing.

"Now listen, Kiddo..." her father began.

"Daddy, that means you too. I'm not kidding."

Hearing a car pull into the driveway, Sarah hoped it would be A.J. and Terri so they could be the buffer between her parents and Sam. Peeking out the kitchen window she was disappointed to see it was Sam. *Oh my God. Where are Terri and A.J.? They promised me they'd be here early.*

CHAPTER THIRTY-ONE

"Ok, so Sam's here, now remember what I said."

Sam arrived in perfect fashion, flowers for Sarah and her mother and a bottle of scotch for her father. *Point for Sam,* thought Sarah with relief.

"Mr. and Mrs. Roberts, it's a real pleasure to meet you both under better circumstances. Mr. Roberts, how are you feeling now? You are one tough guy to have pulled off only a few broken ribs and a minor concussion after that bookcase fell on you and hitting your head on the coffee table."

Another point for Sam. I think he's moving in for the 'kill' to win over my parents and he's succeeding judging by the look on their faces. Sarah observed and smiled.

"Sam, how lovely to meet you again. Thank you so much for the flowers. How very thoughtful of you."

"Mom, let's go into the kitchen and I'll find you a vase for those." Sarah grabbed her mother by the arm and left the living room.

With Karen and Sarah out of hearing range, George was able to have 'words' with Sam.

"Sam, I would like to thank you for how you helped me and my family the night of the accident. I appreciate everything you did."

"It was no trouble, Sir. I was just doing my job." Sam's modesty impressed George.

"You do your job well then, Son." George remained serious. He liked the boy but was still apprehensive. "Now, Sam, I want to speak to you about Sarah…"

"Mr. Roberts, before you begin, I want to assure you that your daughter is safe with me, not that she isn't perfectly capable of taking care of herself…" *Believe me I found that out the hard way,* "She certainly doesn't need me to do that for her and I'm sure much of the thanks goes to you for that. I want you to know that my intentions are honourable, Sir. Now I know she had a rough go with that Travis guy, but I can assure you it won't happen with me." Sam tried to head Mr. Roberts off at the pass.

Listening to Sam, George was quiet and let him say what he needed to. He seemed like a good kid but George still had a few things to say.

"I appreciate that," George paused for effect. "Now I'm going to cut to the chase with you, Son. I want to be sure we have an understanding here." Again George paused. "I'm sure you're a very admirable young man but let me assure you that if you *do* hurt my daughter I'll teach you a lesson you won't soon forget. My daughter is my pride and joy and God help you if you mess with her heart like that son-of-a-bitch Trav..."

Just then Sarah and Karen returned to the living room with drinks for all. Sarah looked carefully from her father to Sam checking to see if there were any problems. Both men were smiling which was hopeful. *I'm guessing Daddy has been behaving himself, thank God.*

"So, what have you guys been talking about?" Sarah asked cautiously, more to check up on her father than anything else.

Looking at each other knowingly, Sam could see that George wanted no part of his daughter in on the conversation that just took place between them so Sam threw him a lifeline.

"I was just about to ask your father if he would like to come by the fire hall tomorrow for a tour and maybe even a ride-a-long." Sam looked over at George knowing he was saving his ass and winked.

Smart-ass. The kid's a smart-ass, but I like him. George looked at Sam with narrowed eyes, knowing what he was up to.

"And I would like that very much, Son. Thank you." *Okay kid you're off the hook. But I'll still be keeping close tabs on you.* When all was said and done, George really did have a good feeling about Sam and was much more comfortable having his daughter dating him over Travis; not that he had any say in the matter anyway.

Once Terri and A.J., arrived they all sat down to dinner followed by an evening full of fun and laughter. The entire room roared at Sam's expense when they heard about all his misadventures with Sarah.

Sarah was relieved that her parents had behaved themselves with no inappropriate questions or comments the entire evening. *In fact, it's almost unbelievable,* she thought with scepticism.

"Well folks, I need to head out. I have to be at the fire hall tomorrow for a tour with another department looking to build a new hall and since ours is the newest one around right now, they decided to come check it out. George, why don't you come by around one o'clock tomorrow and I'll take you on a tour and with any luck, a fire call."

George shook Sam's hand and leaned in quietly. "I owe you one for not telling Sarah I spoke to you and, just to be clear, I think my daughter is in good hands but I'll still be keeping my eye on you, Son."

"Yes sir, there's no doubt in my mind." Sam liked George. He told it like it was and Sam respected that.

After Sam said goodnight to everyone Sarah walked him to the door pleased the evening had gone so well.

"I'll call you tomorrow night, Sarah." Then giving her a goodnight kiss, Sam was on his way.

Walking back into the living room Sarah was thinking through the evening and slowly beginning to put the pieces together.

"Wow, Mom, Dad, you didn't ask one inappropriate question nor embarrass me with Sam all evening long. I'm shocked, really."

"Well dear, you did ask us to stay out of it and we did, isn't that right George?"

"Yeah well, Mom, I don't believe it for a second." Sarah couldn't contain her cynicism.

"Sarah, why so suspicious of your parents?" A.J. asked.

"Why A.J.? Because I know them all too well." Turning to her parents she pushed, "So? Which one of you took Sam aside? Come on. I know one of you did. You know I'll find out so you might just as well tell me now." Sarah was teasing more than anything but wasn't at all surprised to have a confession from her mother.

"Okay, okay, dear. So I took Sam aside for just a moment."

"Just as I suspected. What did you talk to him about, Mom?"

"Well, Sarah, I didn't say much. Only that I hoped he was using protection..."

"Mother! You didn't!" Terri and Sarah exclaimed in unison.

"Well, I wanted to be sure my little girl wouldn't get any communicable diseases..." Karen wasn't apologizing for her actions, just stating a fact.

"Oh my God, Mother, I can't believe you!" Sarah was mortified.

"Mom, that's not your place to be discussing that type of thing with Sam." Terri defended her sister's position.

"Karen, I can't believe you would do that to Sarah after she specifically asked us not to intrude." George tried to keep the focus on his wife to ensure his secret stayed safe.

"Oh come on, George! I heard you speak to Sam about Sarah as well. Don't act so innocent." Karen was trying to keep her head above water and deflected the attention over to her husband. "I heard you in the living room talking."

"Daddy?" Sarah turned to her father who was now starting to look a little flustered under the piercing stare of both his daughters and his wife.

"Sarah, I just wanted to make sure he understood the lay of the land, is all, and quite frankly I have a right to..."

"Oh my God, you two are unbelievable! How humiliating! How am I going to be able to face Sam now?" Sarah was horrified.

"Listen Sarah. As far as I'm concerned, Sam deserves to go through this with your father. If I had to then so does he. It's only fair after all. Sam's a big boy; he can handle it." A.J. was completely amused by the entire scenario. Terri just glared at him.

"Yes, but I'm sure my mom never spoke to you about protection, A.J. I mean, honestly, Mother!"

Laughing, A.J. said, "Well, admittedly that wasn't a topic that ever came up..."

"No, but Mother spoke to *me* about it." Terri interjected and with that they all laughed, realizing that it was a losing battle when it came to having Sarah's parents butt out of their daughters' private lives.

Well, better Sam find out now what mom and dad are like before getting too far along into our relationship, thought Sarah with dismay.

When the day finally arrived for her parents to head home Sarah was disappointed that it had gone by faster than she had hoped. She was going to miss them and hated to see them leave.

Standing by the car after her parents had packed up, she gave them both a big hug goodbye.

“Sarah, be sure to thank Sam again for giving me a tour of the fire hall. I can’t tell you how excited I was to go on that call to the barn fire with them. I know I had to stay well out of the way but I must admit that it was one of the most fascinating things I’ve ever witnessed.”

She smiled thinking about how excited her father had been when he returned from the fire hall.

“I told Sam next time I’m in town I would like to take him out for a beer and maybe a little fishing.

Sarah’s mouth dropped open. *Are you kidding me? A few days ago he was practically the enemy and now one trip to the fire hall and her father was practically swooning over Sam and hadn’t stopped talking about him.*

Sarah hugged her mother goodbye and once they were in the car, George added, “I have no worries about this boy, Sarah. You don’t want to lose him. He’s an outstanding young man and I couldn’t have picked a better person for you to be with if I had chosen him myself.”

“Um, okay.” Sarah was dumbfounded.

Wow! Sarah was ecstatic about the change in her father’s attitude. Waving goodbye to them, Sarah sighed with contentment. Shivering, she decided to go in and start a fire in the fireplace. It was early December and although there hadn’t been any snow to speak of, the air was crisp and cool and felt like it could snow any day. She decided it would be the perfect afternoon to just cozy in and read a book before meeting up with Sam in a couple of hours for dinner.

THIRTY-TWO

THE PHONE RINGING INTERRUPTED HER quiet day. Although she hadn't heard from him since Chloe had left Sarah was still concerned it would be Travis calling and let it go to message. Hitting the playback button she reluctantly listened.

"Sarah, are you there?"

"Sarah, I know you're listening."

"Fine, don't fucking answer. I just want you to know that I'm fucking coming for my money. Do you hear me, Sarah? I'm coming for my fucking money so I can fix my fucking car that you fucking destroyed on me, you fucking bitch!"

Once again, he was drunk but what made her more nervous was that he seemed drunker than usual and his anger had escalated drastically. She conceded that she was in over her head now. She had let things go on too long.

Sarah knew it was time to ask for help but couldn't decide whether to ask A.J. or Sam. After some deliberation, she opted to call A.J. *I had better not drag Sam into this; I've caused him enough trouble as it is and besides, A.J. knows Travis all too well.*

She was grateful to have A.J. answer the phone. "Um, hi A.J., is Terri home?"

"No Sarah, she's out doing a house closing. She won't be home until later this evening. Do you want me to have her call you?"

"Uh, no, actually I need your help with something and was wondering if I could come over and talk to you about it?" Sarah tried not to come across sounding worried.

"Sure, is everything alright?"

"It's too much to discuss over the phone. I'll explain when I see you."

He was concerned because Sarah sounded upset but reluctantly conceded to waiting but when she still had not arrived an hour later began to get concerned. Thankfully just then the phone rang.

"Sarah, where are you? I was getting worried."

"A.J. it's me, Sam. I was going to come over for a quick beer before picking Sarah up for dinner at seven. What are you up to?"

"Hey Sam. Well, I've been waiting for Sarah to show up. She phoned me to say she needed my help with something and was supposed to be right over. I'm starting to get a little concerned because she hasn't shown up yet and I can't get her on the phone. Can you stop by her place on your way and see what's going on? I'll wait here in case she shows up."

"Sure A.J., no problem and hey, don't worry, I'm sure she's fine." Sam reassured his friend, although admittedly he was also concerned.

On the way, Sam found Sarah's car broken down at the side of the road with Sarah nowhere in sight. *Well that explains why she isn't at A.J.'s,* he thought. Approaching her car Sam became alarmed. Written all over it were the words 'YOU BITCH'. It was dark so Sam pulled his flashlight out, looked into and walked around the car. Finding Sarah's cell phone broken on the ground, he picked it up. *There's no wonder A.J. couldn't reach her.* Sam now regretted forgetting his own cell phone at home. He feared that this was much more than Sarah just being late and quickly headed to her house.

Pulling into Sarah's driveway, he saw another car. Flashlight in hand, he saw that it was a rental. Walking up to the house Sam noticed the side door wide open and quietly stepped into the kitchen. It was then that he heard Sarah's desperate plea coming from the direction of her bedroom.

"Why are you doing this to me, Travis?"

What the hell is he doing here? It was obvious something was wrong and like any good firefighter, decided the best tactic was to deal with the situation head on. However, running down the hall and into the bedroom, Sam got more than he bargained for.

The last thing he heard before losing consciousness was, "That must be your new boyfriend coming to save the day, Baby."

Not hearing from Sam, A.J. decided it was time to get involved. Grabbing his gun, A.J. was grateful Terri was out closing a house deal so she wouldn't worry. He wasn't sure what was going on but he sure as hell was going to find out.

Coming upon Sarah's car at the side of the road, A.J. did a quick security check, then notified the station that he was heading directly to Sarah's and asked that officers standby should he require further assistance. All signs indicated there was something seriously wrong and although his professionalism guided him through the natural process of what he should do, inside he was worried about Sarah, and now Sam.

Approaching Sarah's house, A.J. saw Sam's truck in the driveway as well as a rental car. He decided to call the license plate into the station and have it run through the system. Parking and getting out of his car, A.J. drew his gun and walked cautiously and quietly up to the house. The side door was wide open without a soul in sight. Once inside the kitchen, A.J. heard Sarah's frantic voice from the bedroom.

"Oh my God! Oh my God!"

Then he heard another familiar voice replying, "Holy shit! Now look what happened! I said you'd pay for what you did Sarah but it wasn't supposed go down this way and now your boyfriend's probably dead, thanks to you!"

"Oh my God, Sam! Please wake up!"

That was all A.J. needed to hear as he stormed the bedroom, gun at the ready, screaming, "Police! Drop your weapons!" However, nothing could have prepared A.J. for what he was about to see and when he finally acknowledged what was going on, he wasn't quite sure how to react.

Sam was unconscious on the floor with Sarah kneeling down trying to revive him, but what was most surprising was seeing Travis tied up with bungee cords in a chair with a black and blue 'goose egg' on his forehead. *What the hell?*

Looking up at A.J., Travis calmly said, "Oh, hey A.J., long time no see. How's it goin'?"

Raising his eyebrows in amazement, A.J. looked from Travis to Sarah and asked, "Sarah what the hell is going on?"

Travis quickly jumped in, "You want to know what's going on A.J.? I'll tell you what's going on. That sister-in-law of yours is one crazy bitch who needs to learn to control her temper and think before she acts! Holy shit, she's a raving lunatic! You need to do something about her!"

CHAPTER THIRTY-TWO

"Shuddup, Travis! I didn't ask you." responded A.J. trying to absorb what he was seeing. He wasn't quite sure what to think at this point.

"Oh my God A.J.! It's poor Sam, I think he came to rescue me, or something but quite frankly, he wasn't doing a very good job of it if you ask me. I mean who the hell comes running up behind a girl in a crisis yelling, 'I'll get you, Sarah!' I mean really, what's a girl to think? I thought he was attacking me and so I turned around and slugged him in the head with my baseball bat and knocked him out and honestly A.J. I didn't mean to do it…well, I did mean to, but I didn't know it was him until it was too late and holy shit, if he survives, he's going to hate me, or kill me, or both and you know we just started dating and, oh my God A.J., I'm so sorry!" Sarah was almost out of breath when she finished and was relieved to hear Sam moan and try to get up.

"Sarah, you're fucking out of your mind! First you slug me over the head and tie me up and then your boyfriend here…"

"Shut up, Travis or I'll slug you again!" Sarah had just about enough of this night.

"Whoa, A.J.! Are you gonna let her threaten me like that?" Travis asked indignantly.

"Shuddup, Travis!" replied A.J., putting his gun away.

A.J. offered a hand up to Sam, who was rubbing the side of his head and sluggishly asked, "What the hell happened?"

Travis grabbed his opportunity to be heard once again and announced, "I'll tell you what happened pal! Your girlfriend here fucking slugged you over the head with a baseball bat and quite frankly you can have her, I'm glad to be rid of her! She's one crazy bitch!"

Sarah glared at Travis, grabbed the bat and stood up but A.J. grabbed her arm and stopped her.

"Sit down, Sarah, and tell me what the hell is going on." By now A.J. was completely confused and curiosity was starting to get the best of him. Just then confirmation came through on the rental car and A.J. responded, "10-4 Sergeant. No need for assistance at this time." Turning to Sarah A.J. awaited her response.

Sitting down on the edge of the bed Sarah began to enlighten him.

"A.J., it all started when my car broke down. I dropped my cell phone, which broke, and had to walk back home to call you but when I got home Travis had broken into my house..."

"The hell I had sweetheart! I simply came to let you know that I saw your car at the side of the road and that I left a note on it like the one you left on mine, and then you bloody well took a baseball bat to my head!"

"Is that what happened to me?" Sam asked, still dazed and rubbing his head.

"Yeah, Pal! That's exactly what happened to you! I told you, she's fucking nuts!" Travis eagerly jumped in.

"Shuddup, Travis!" A.J. was irritated.

Sarah continued, "So, as I was saying, Travis had broken in and I was terrified because I heard someone in my house. So I snuck into the living room and grabbed my baseball bat. I keep it by the chair, just in case. I could hear him sneaking around in my bedroom, so I quietly walked in and slugged the intruder on the head with it. The lights were out, it was dark and I couldn't see who it was but, if I had...well...I still would have slugged him on the head...only harder!"

"You bitch!" Travis retaliated.

"Shut the hell up, Travis!" A.J. yelled.

CHAPTER THIRTY-TWO

"Anyway, when I turned the light on and saw it was Travis, I grabbed the bungee cords and tied him up. He's been stalking me since we broke up and I was afraid of what he would do. That's what I was coming to talk to you about tonight."

With raised eyebrows, A.J. glared at Travis who squirmed in the chair, uncomfortable under A.J.'s scrutinizing stare.

"What!? She bloody well ruined my car, A.J.! You should see it! It's going to cost a fortune to get it repainted!" Travis defended himself.

"Travis, how in hell could you stalk Sarah living two hours away? And besides, don't you have better things to do with your time, like play football?" A.J. asked.

Uncomfortable, Travis wasn't sure whether he should answer or not.

"Answer the question, Travis. You know I'm going to find out eventually." A.J. sternly insisted.

Clearing his throat Travis answered, "I have a buddy who lives in the area. I asked him to keep an eye on Sarah and what she was up to. He was feeding me the information. He's actually the one who came across Sarah's car and called me so I told him to leave the note on her car for me because I was already at her house and figured it was the perfect opportunity to show her what it feels like to have your car ruined." At this point Travis didn't care that he was incriminating himself.

"What?!" Sarah felt her privacy even more violated than before.

"Unbelievable. Well, I suppose I'll have to have words with your buddy too then. What's his name?"

"I'm not giving you his name A.J. I want him left out of this."

I'm shocked over this small semblance of loyalty coming from Travis. Seems out of character, thought A.J.

"Does this guy not work?" A.J. asked

"Naw, he was fired a few months ago and he needed a few bucks, so I paid him to follow Sarah around. I didn't mean anything by it. Just trying to scare her a little." Travis defended. "Besides she started all of this, A.J. She should never have marked up my Beamer."

Shaking his head in disbelief, A.J. turned to Sarah, "Go on."

"Anyway, next thing I know I heard Sam, although I didn't know it was Sam until it was too late, and he came running in sounding like a crazy man and well, one thing led to another and…oh my God, this is such a nightmare!" Sarah sat down on the bed and dropped her face into both her hands.

"A nightmare? For who? I'm the one whose Beamer needs repainting and I'm the one tied up here with a friggin' concussion!" shouted Travis grasping for sympathy.

Sam had a splitting headache, but after listening to Sarah talk, he was slowly beginning to acknowledge what had taken place and wasn't happy.

"Are you bloody well kidding me? You mean to say that you slugged me over the head with a baseball bat when I was coming to rescue you? Who does that?"

"Yeah, well…" Travis interrupted. "If you think you've got it bad pal you should see my Beamer! She wrote all over it in black marker and I'd just finished detailing it, man! That bitch has got one nasty temper! I'm telling you, she's fucking dangerous!"

Yeah, I'm hearing ya pal. Sam quietly sympathized with the dangerous part.

"Well...guess what, Sarah? I don't want you back now! Your boyfriend here can have you. I was going to give you a second chance but you can't expect a guy to take you back when you slug him over the head with a baseball bat and write all over his Beamer. We're through, Sarah!" shouted Travis resentfully.

"Oh my God, you've got to be kidding me! I'm telling you for the last time, I don't want to get back with you, Travis!" Sarah rolled her eyes and flopped back onto her bed staring at the ceiling in frustration.

"A.J., I have to agree with Travis here about Sarah...no one's safe when she's around, especially me!" Sam joked.

"Sam!" Sarah cried sitting back up.

Looking at Sarah, Sam grinned then winked in her direction.

Rolling her eyes, Sarah flopped backwards onto her bed again.

"Or me, don't forget...I think she did some serious damage. I need to see a doctor for chrissakes!" added Travis.

A.J. just watched and listened in complete astonishment as all three of them continued talking at once. He was getting more irritated by the moment.

"Okay, I want all three of you to shut the hell up right NOW!" he bellowed above the chatter.

Everyone immediately stopped talking, knowing that when A.J. was irritated it was best not to push him.

Silence fell in the room.

Finally, some peace and quiet, thought A.J. *I'm in a bloody nut house!* Contemplating what to do next, A.J. couldn't believe the circus act that was unfolding before him and wondered how the hell he was going to explain it back at the station.

Daring to break through the wall of silence, a voice brazenly asked…

“Uh...hello…? Is someone going to untie me or what?”

“Shuddup, Travis!” Sarah, Sam, and A.J. all shouted at once.

THIRTY-THREE

After some deliberation, A.J. decided what needed to be done. “Okay, so until I can figure out what the hell I want to do about all of this, this is what’s going to happen. Sarah, take Sam to the hospital and get him checked out by a doctor. Travis here is going to go with me to the station and enjoy a night in jail, compliments of the Forestville Police…”

“WHAT! Are you kidding me A.J.? I need a doctor too you know and besides I didn’t do anything wrong here. I was just helping your sister-in-law understand the error of her ways! Why the hell do I have to go to jail for that? I’m the victim here. It’s *my* fucking Beamer she destroyed!” Travis’ plea of wrongful injustice fell on deaf ears.

“Travis, I highly recommend you shut the hell up once and for all or I’m going to have you charged with mischief, stalking, break and enter, criminal harassment...would you like me to go on or do you catch my drift?” A.J. was losing what little patience he had left.

Travis knew not to push A.J., although wanting to show that he didn’t approve of any of it muttered under his breath and shook his head disapprovingly, knowing well enough to keep his mouth shut.

With that, A.J. untied Travis and threw handcuffs on him, then called the station to say that everything was under control and he was heading into the station with a prisoner.

Sarah and Sam left for the hospital and A.J. walked Travis out to the police car, placed him in the back seat and headed to the police station. He was getting more tired and more miserable by the minute.

"You know, A.J., Sarah is a bit of a loose cannon. I mean who in their right mind writes all over a Beamer in permanent black marker? A Beamer! You can understand my dilemma? I mean it was uncalled for! Yeah okay, I was seeing the cheerleader, and yeah, I saw her once or twice...well, okay...a few times, but, hey, it wasn't serious, just a fling. It's Sarah I loved. With Gretchen it was just...well...it was just...sex! You know what it's like A.J. I mean she threw herself at me and she's fucking hot and well, how could I turn her down? Sarah just took it too personally. She took it way too far. I offered to take her back but you know Sarah...she's stubborn, A.J., and well, there was just no reasoning with her. And I ask you, why did she have to drag my Beamer into this?"

Travis rambled the entire drive back to the police station which was grating on A.J.'s nerves. He had just about enough of Travis' rambling for one night. Getting out of the car, Travis continued to ramble, so up the walkway to the door of the station A.J. discretely stuck his foot out in front of Travis who tripped and fell flat on his face.

Finally, he shuts the hell up, thought A.J. *Just a little bit of payback for what he did to Sarah,* he smiled.

To Travis, A.J. barked, "What the hell, Travis, have you been drinking too?" and roughly helped him back to his feet again.

"NO, I haven't been drinking you fucking asshole!" Travis wasn't sure what happened but suspected he'd had help going down.

CHAPTER THIRTY-THREE

"Sergeant, have the prisoner checked out by a doctor and then book him BTAS!", A.J. barked the order out and handed Travis over. The officer knowingly smiled and said, "No problem, Chief."

BTAS was their station's in-house acronym for 'Book The Asshole Slowly'. It was then understood that this guy had been giving a hard time to the charging officer and they were to take their sweet time booking him in, including prints, mug shot, breathalyser, drug testing, the works. Then A.J. ordered them to lock Travis up until he was back the next morning. A.J. wanted to be sure Sarah had no more trouble from Travis tonight and besides, he honestly wasn't sure what to do about Travis, or the entire situation for that matter. *The whole thing is absolutely unbelievable!* A.J. fumed on the way back home knowing he had to sleep on this one to be able to gain some perspective.

THIRTY-FOUR

THE NEXT MORNING, A.J. WAS up later than usual. Yawning, he walked into the kitchen but Terri had already left for work. Pouring himself a coffee, he sat at the kitchen table still deliberating over the entire chain of events from the night before. Hearing the phone ring he looked on the display to see who was calling and answered with impatience. "What is it, Sergeant?"

"Sir, what should we do about the prisoner?"

"I'll be in the station shortly, Sergeant, what's the problem?" A.J. really wasn't in the mood to discuss Travis.

"Sir, he's driving us all crazy here! He won't shut the hell up and now he's demanding to be charged or released." Sergeant Morris went on to explain that the prisoner hadn't slept all night long and kept yelling from his cell that he was the victim. "He keeps saying that he wants justice, a lawyer, his one phone call." Sergeant Morris was sounding uncharacteristically flustered.

"Morris, since when can't you deal with a simple prisoner making a bit of noise?"

"Oh, he's not your average prisoner, Chief. Since I started shift at 0600 hours he has repeated the same thing over and over again. 'I want justice for my Beamer, I want justice for my Beamer, I want justice for my Beamer, I want just…'"

"I get the picture, Sergeant." A.J. rolled his eyes. *Travis always was an asshole.*

"Sir, it's been three hours! Can we at least charge him with disturbing the peace?" the Sergeant asked frantically.

"As tempting as it may be Sergeant, no we can't. I'll head into the station shortly but in the meantime tell the prisoner if he doesn't shut the hell up that you'll lock him up in solitary where no one can hear his sorry ass!" and with that A.J. slammed down the phone, grabbed his keys and headed over to see Sam.

♡ ♡ ♡

Arriving at Sam's, A.J. walked into the house announcing to his friend that he was there. Noticing the mouth-watering aroma of bacon in the air, A.J. headed straight to the kitchen. Seeing Sarah A.J. sighed. *She's the other one I have to deal with.*

"Oh…ah…hey A.J. I stayed with Sam last night…" Unsure what to say next, Sarah looked down at the cooking bacon and back at A.J. and sheepishly asked, "Do you want some breakfast?" Judging by the look on A.J.'s face, she suspected she was in big trouble with him.

"Sarah, we need to talk." "Sit down."

Sarah cringed, wiped her hands with a hand towel and sat down at the kitchen table opposite A.J. Scrunching up her face Sarah started, "A.J., I can explain…"

CHAPTER THIRTY-FOUR

"No, let me do the talking." A.J. was still irritated and had no interest in small talk. "First of all Sarah…" *Where the hell do I begin?* Looking out the window he saw ducks floating on the pond and the water sparkling in the sunshine. Turning his attention back to Sarah, he sighed heavily.

"First of all, did you get your car towed to Old Bill's so he can fix it up for you?"

"Yes, this morning." Sarah dreaded where the conversation was going.

"Okay, good."

Sitting quietly for a moment A.J. finally asked, "What the hell were you thinking, Sarah? You could have been hurt not to mention you almost put both Sam and Travis into the hospital. Not that I give a rat's ass about Travis but why in hell wouldn't you have told me from the beginning that Travis was giving you trouble? That's what I'm here for!" Once he started, he couldn't stop.

"My God, Sarah, trouble seems to follow you; first Sam's truck; now Travis. Is there anything else I should know about because now's the time to tell me. Your sister is going to kill me when she finds out what happened. She's going to wonder how I could let this happen and you know what I'm going to tell her? Well…do you?"

Sarah meekly shook her head no. She had never seen A.J. so upset before and knew enough to keep quiet.

"I'm going to bloody well tell her that her sister doesn't know enough to control her temper and that her sister is going to fix all of this once and for all and that her sister isn't going to cause anymore trouble. Understand, Sarah?" A.J. was red-faced and his voice grew louder the more he talked. Sarah just nodded in agreement, allowing him to get it out of his system.

"Now, let me tell you what is going to happen next."

Sarah almost whispered when she said, "Ok..." and waited for A.J. to continue.

"First of all, once you are done sucking up to Sam with this breakfast idea of yours, which sadly will work, you are going to tell your sister what happened and you are going to be sure she is perfectly clear that it has been resolved, that you will not be hearing from Travis anymore and you had damn well better make sure that none of this comes back to haunt me as far as Terri is concerned." A.J. had to stop to take a much-needed breath.

"Secondly, I'm going to go down to the police station this morning and tell Travis that no charges will be laid against you for the damages to his car because you won't be laying any charges against him for mischief, criminal harassment, break and enter, or anything else that stupid bastard has done to piss me off. Then he is going to leave town and never bother you again..." A.J. stopped momentarily. "...and last but not least Sarah, you are going to be a model citizen..."

"And don't forget about making it up to Sam for slugging him and almost ruining his rugged good looks, not to mention creating unnecessary anxiety for someone so awesome."

They hadn't noticed Sam walking into the kitchen to pour himself a coffee. Taking a whiff of the bacon, Sam added, "I'm thinking a breakfast like this is a good start to making it up to me, though."

Grinning, Sam used the towel tossed around his shoulders to give his hair one last dry and threw it down on the counter. Grabbing a piece of bacon he sat down at the table and leaned back in his chair. *What a sight these two are.* He chuckled at the sight of A.J. so angry and Sarah looking pathetically like a little kid in trouble with her parents. *Boy, this bacon hits the spot.*

"You know A.J., I think all in all Sarah handled herself pretty well. I mean she didn't know what was going on last night and in all fairness to her, she did try to come over to see you. Aren't you glad to know that she can defend herself, albeit all too well," he said, rubbing the bump on his head.

"I don't think you can hold all of this against her. I think she had every right to handle things the way she did…okay, other than hitting me over the head with a baseball bat of course and well I must admit, marking up the Beamer wasn't so nice. If I were Travis I'd be pissed off too but I mean the guy just took everything way too far. The guy's an asshole, A.J., and he got what he deserved and as far as Sarah and I are concerned...well, we don't need you to sort that out for us…anymore. We already figured it out all by ourselves, Boss."

Sam threw that last word in for effect because he knew it would anger A.J. Even as kids, whenever A.J. tried to take over and organize things, Sam would give him a hard time and would inevitably end up calling A.J. boss and A.J. grew to hate it. With a cheeky grin, Sam chuckled to himself as he watched Sarah sit in disbelief, thankfully quiet for once and A.J. giving him the, 'I want to punch that smart ass grin off your face for calling me boss.' look. But without giving A.J. or Sarah a chance to say another word, Sam leaned back, crossed his feet up on the kitchen table, took a sip of his coffee and asked, "So…can we eat or what? I'm starving!"

THIRTY-FIVE

"What the hell? Are you kidding me? Not lay charges? Do you seriously think I'm going to apologize to that bitch?"

"Well to start with, Travis, if you call Sarah that one more time, I'll take you into a room without a security camera and punch you in the face! Secondly, you have no choice, my man. It's that or you will be charged with mischief, stalking, criminal harassment, break and enter and, if I could, I would have you charged with stupidity, but there's no law against that yet. I'm also willing to forget about your buddy in this whole scenario, but you had better make damn sure he knows to leave Sarah alone or I'll track down who he is and then throw you both in jail. So, I recommend you cut your losses pal and head back home before it gets really nasty for you."

"What about the damages to my Beamer? Do you know how much that's going to cost to have a new paint job done, A.J.? That bitc..." Travis thought twice about his words and continued, "...that sister-in-law of yours used Goddamned permanent black marker on it. There is no getting that shit off! That's going to cost me a small fortune to fix..." Stopping, Travis could see that he was getting nowhere with A.J.

"So what is it, Travis, a new paint job and jail for you and your friend or are you going to shut the hell up, go home and never bother Sarah again?"

Travis was smart enough to realize this was a no-win situation and although still frustrated, agreed to leave, but refused to apologize. He was completely livid and grabbed his belongings from Sergeant Morris in such a huff that they dropped all over the floor. Muttering an expletive as he picked everything up Travis then headed out of the station, but decided that he wanted to get one last 'word' in before he left.

Stopping at the doorway, he turned around and with a scowl flipped A.J. his middle finger. Seeing A.J. reach for his handcuffs and head towards him, the look on Travis' face quickly changed from cocky to scared and in his rush to leave he lost his balance and tripped. With an expletive or two he caught his balance, clasped his belongings tighter to his chest and scurried hastily out the door. Watching the whole scene unfold, A.J. and Sergeant Morris laughed aloud and then went about their business.

THIRTY-SIX

THE SITUATION WITH TRAVIS LONG behind her, Sarah was finally able to relax and enjoy her new home and her exciting romance with Sam. Gratefully, A.J.'s little 'talk' with Travis seemed to work and he never bothered her again. Life seemed to be getting back on track once more.

It was Christmas Eve and Sarah was thrilled her parents were coming to spend the holidays at Terri and A.J.'s. At Terri's suggestion, Sarah invited Sam and Old Bill to join them for Christmas dinner since neither had any family to speak of.

Sam had asked Sarah to spend Christmas Eve with him. Apparently, the shelter needed help feeding the pups once more before they went to their forever homes. Sadly, Sam told her that all the pups were spoken for and although Sarah was disappointed she decided in the New Year to check out other dogs in the shelter to look at adopting one of them instead. Hearing Sam pull into her driveway Sarah put on her hat, grabbed her coat and gloves and ran out to meet him.

Getting into his truck, Sarah was pretty excited about her first parade in Forestville, especially after all her efforts recruiting floats. She was especially proud of getting Joe's Hardware to put his first float in and was interested to see what he came up with.

“Hi, Sam. Thanks for picking me up. This will be so much fun going to an evening parade. I’m sure it will be so pretty.”

“The committee even has their own spot reserved in the middle of town because we have to judge the floats and pick our top three choices to win. Every year it’s the same groups who win, so hopefully, with you managing to get some new businesses participating, there will be a bit more competition this year.”

The parade went without a hitch, with the top float managing to surprise everyone. Joe beamed from ear to ear when it was announced Joe’s Hardware won first prize.

“Thank you very much. I have no idea why everyone doesn’t put a float into the parade. It’s not a lot of money to participate and…”

Listening to Joe speak to the newspaper reporter, it was at this point that the committee decided to leave for the Old Beagle to grab a few drinks before heading home.

“What a bunch of bullshit. That cheap bastard always said it was too much money to put a float in the parade,” Geoff said as he ordered a beer.

“Don’t let it bother you, Geoff. The guy’s an asshole and everyone in town knows it. Let him have his moment in the spotlight.” Sam chuckled.

Sitting down beside Sarah, Bill asked, “So Sam told me that yer friend Chloe is going to move ta Forestville. When is she movin’?”

“Well, there were a few delays in selling her house and she needed to wrap things up there first. She’s expects to move early in the New Year though.” Looking over at Geoff she saw him smile warmly as he overheard the conversation. *I guess he really does like her.* Sarah knew that Chloe and Geoff had been talking to each other almost daily since she left and just to tease him, Sarah added, "Isn't that right Geoff?"

"Oh, yes, that's right…I guess. I dunno." Geoff recovered fairly quickly, not wanting to expose his deep interest in Chloe.

Sarah and Sam laughed knowingly but decided not to push him too much because, in fact, neither of them had seen their friends so happy or content than since meeting each other. They were pleased with the way things were working out for Chloe and Geoff.

"By the way, where are A.J. and Terri? Weren't they supposed to come back for drinks?" Geoff changed the subject as quickly as possible.

"They were going to but my mom and dad are arriving at some point this evening and they needed to be home for them." Sarah could hardly wait to see her parents.

Almost forgetting to pass the message on, Sam shouted, "But A.J. said the drinks were on him tonight so drink up boys! He also said that in the New Year there will be a dinner at his place for everyone who helped on the parade committee."

"Will you pass that onto the kid, Bill? Where is he anyway? Didn't he show up to help tonight?" Sam couldn't remember seeing Will around.

"Yup, he sure did, Sam. Ole Will was on poop clean-up duty after the horses in the parade." Bill laughed. "The kid was pissed as he could be with me but he did 'er. I asked him if he wanted ta join us here but he said he was meeting up with his friends afterwards. I told him ta git his ass ta my shop bright and early after the New Year. I'm open next week but thought I would give him the week off."

"Well, that's more than he deserved, Bill, but it was nice of you to do that for him." Rudy offered.

"Aw, he's not a bad kid, just a bit of a shit disturber. I can see a bit of myself in him. After his six months of community service are done I'll see if he wants ta come work fer me apprenticing. He's pretty good with the cars. I think he could be a fine mechanic some day. Sometimes we all deserve ta catch a break when we make mistakes," Bill smiled with understanding.

After a couple of beers and much conversation, Sam decided it was time to head out.

"Merry Christmas, folks! Sarah and I need to go feed some puppies before the night is over. Geoff, you want to come along and help clean out pens, Buddy?" Sam winked at Geoff who scoffed at him.

"Yeah, right! I don't think so but thanks anyway."

Laughing, Sam shook everyone's hands and Sarah gave them all a hug wishing them Merry Christmas.

"Bill, we'll see you tomorrow at Terri and A.J.'s for dinner."

"Looking forward to it, Sammy boy." Bill raised his glass of beer in response.

Leaving the Old Beagle and heading to the shelter, Sarah was surprised to see Sam head to his place instead.

"I thought we had to go to the shelter to feed pups, Sam? Why are you heading to your place?" Sarah was confused.

"We do, but I need to pick something up at home first. It'll only take a moment."

Walking into Sam's place Sarah took off her boots and watched Sam disappear towards the bedroom. Sitting down on the couch in the kitchen Sarah patted Benny who was curled up contentedly sleeping on the one end.

CHAPTER THIRTY-SIX

From the bedroom, Sam called out, "Sarah, close your eyes. I have a surprise for you." Smiling, she presumed Sam had decided to give her a Christmas present and was eager to see what it was. She could hear Benny whine and heard him hop off the couch and run off. Feeling Sam sit down on the couch beside her, Sarah could hardly contain her excitement.

"Come on Sam, what are you doing? What is it?"

"Okay, Sarah. Open your eyes."

Opening them, Sarah immediately began to cry. Sitting beside her on the couch was not only Sam but also the blonde retriever pup she had so desperately wanted to adopt. Looking up at Sam questioningly, he smiled.

"She's all yours, Sarah. Merry Christmas."

"Oh my God, Sam! I thought you said all the pups were spoken for." Sam passed her to Sarah who laughed as the pup immediately began to lick her face, tail wagging furiously.

"They *were* all spoken for. I just didn't tell you that it was me who had spoken for this little cutie."

Tears of joy were rolling down Sarah's cheeks. Holding the pup she leaned in towards Sam and kissed him.

"Thank you so much, Sam. This is the nicest surprise I've ever had. I don't know what to say really. I'm so happy."

"Well, you'll have to come up with a name. I'll help you get things set up at your place for her. I bought everything you need: leash, toys, crate, bowls, and food. You can just take her home and enjoy her which I'm sure Benny will be happy about. He hasn't been too pleased about having a rambunctious pup around here today."

Looking over at Benny lying on the floor, looking rather hurt that the pup was getting all the attention, Sarah called to him but he refused to come over. She could only assume it was because of the pup.

"I wonder if Benny will ever be happy about me bringing this puppy around to visit," she pondered.

"Well, I'm hoping that maybe one day you won't have to bring the puppy just to visit. Perhaps one day it can be a more...permanent arrangement." Sam optimistically suggested.

Sarah's attention was quickly drawn away from the puppy to look over at Sam. Putting the pup on the floor, Sarah watched as she ran over to Benny and started jumping all over him trying to get him to play. Taken by surprise, she wasn't sure how to respond to Sam's suggestion. A sense of panic began to set in. After everything she had been through with Travis her gut reaction was to immediately say no.

Sam quickly regretted what he said. *She's taking too long to respond. This was clearly a mistake.*

"Listen Sarah, I'm sorry..."

"No. Wait." Sarah interrupted allowing herself additional time to think.

Sam couldn't help but reprimand himself. *I should have waited.*

Sarah hesitated while putting careful thought to what she was about to say. "Listen Sam..." Sighing aloud she momentarily bit down on her lip then nervously continued, "Well...I want you to know that...I really hope so too." Then quietly revelled in the realization that she genuinely felt the same way.

Relief swept over him.

"Okay. Good," was all he could muster as he smiled with a nod.

CHAPTER THIRTY-SIX

Wanting to ease the awkwardness of the moment Sarah said, "Hey, don't we have some puppies to feed?"

"Nope. No pups to feed. They all went to their forever homes today." Sam felt rather pleased that he had managed to pull off the big surprise without Sarah suspecting a thing.

"I see." Sarah laughed. "Well, you have no idea how happy I am right now. This little pup is absolutely adorable. I'm not sure what I should name her though." Putting some thought to it Sarah said, "Since her eyes are such a dark brown I think I like the name, Brownie."

"Okay then, Brownie it is. So what do you say we head over to your sister's place? I do believe they are waiting on us for a late dinner and I'm starving."

"You mean they all know about this?"

"They sure do, so let's go introduce Brownie to her extended family, shall we?"